I0548884

Dear Miklos

Dear Miklos

Victoria Bastedo

Black Lyon Publishing, LLC

DEAR MIKLOS
Copyright © 2012 by Victoria Bastedo

All rights reserved. No part of this book may be used or reproduced in any way by any means without the written permission of the publisher, except in the case of brief quotations embodied in critical articles and reviews.

Please note that if you have purchased this book without a cover or in any way marked as an advance reading copy, you have purchased a stolen item, and neither the author nor the publisher has been compensated for their work.

Our books may be ordered through your local bookstore or by visiting the publisher:

www.BlackLyonPublishing.com

Black Lyon Publishing, LLC
PO Box 567
Baker City, OR 97814

This is a work of fiction. All of the characters, names, events, organizations and conversations in this novel are either the products of the author's vivid imagination or are used in a fictitious way for the purposes of this story.

Cover Model: Jason Aaron Baca
Cover Photo: Craig Williams

ISBN-10:   1-934912-47-6
ISBN-13:   978-1-934912-47-8
Library of Congress Control Number: 2012940545

Published and printed in
the United States of America.

Black Lyon Contemporary Romance

For Mary Stewart, and her book, The Moonspinners,
published fifty years ago in 1962.
I wrote Dear Miklos *as a tribute.*

Chapter One

I wrote the first letter to him when I was ten years old. After all, he'd saved my life. My mother and I had flown to Greece for a holiday, and because of him I returned home safe again to Seattle. In my mind's eye I could see him every time I pulled out my paper and my pen. His heavy black waves of hair cut short against the straight bone structure of his face, the brown skin of his back, and the lively expression in his dark brown eyes. On frosty mornings in the Montana winters, where we would go to visit distant family between Thanksgiving and Christmas, that vision of his slim sturdy back against the Cretan sunshine would warm me. In the muggy Seattle summers, during the rare times when the temperature would climb above ninety-five, the sparkle of the waterdrops on his cheek and his brown waist and arms would refresh me. He was golden to me, forever twelve-years-old and joyful.

He answered all of my letters, too. I wonder now what he must have thought of them, the regularly arriving little envelopes, with stamps I chose because of the pictures, and small drawings of hearts or butterflies on the part of the envelope that made a tip in the back. He responded through the rest of my little girlhood, during the questioning and yearning of early-teen confusion, and the determined bustle at the end of adolescence. Did he show my letters to his friends, bragging about his one-girl fan club from the United States?

My letters were long, telling him about what those near me said and my responses. They were full of my odd sense of humor, dry and delighted with the ridiculous. Often I would describe every book I was reading, whether it was schoolwork or happy fiction. Even now, at twenty-two, I find myself telling him about everything

I'm reading.

But in recent times the tone of my letters has changed. I haven't been able to tell him much about my troubles. Crete is a colorful place, where the light blue of the sky is just as bright as the dark blue jewel tones of the sea. The sand is gold, and the stone is white. I've always escaped there, in my letters to him; my friend who I knew for three weeks in the summer of 1963. He was the twelve-year-old who tolerated me when I followed his shadow that holiday. He answered all of my questions in his melodious English, and then answered slow in his own language with a laugh when I tried to speak in Greek. He showed me caves and shells, scolded me when I swam out too far, and then, finally, he jumped in the water and saved my life. It's funny but I remember what I was wearing that day, my new bright pink wrap-around shirt with the ruffles, and my pure white sailor shorts.

We never spoke of how I ended up in the water. I'd been thrown in because of the catapult of a speedboat taking off, plunged off the side as it arced and sped away with a sudden roar. My mother had laughed, not knowing that I was no longer silent in the back corner, with the orange life preserver around my neck. That man she was dating then didn't like having to take a ten-year-old everywhere they went. I was an awkward interruption of his time, and his desire. The life preserver, too big and loose, had remained on the surface when I sunk below it. And, as its string was tangled on a white cluster of rope at the back of the boat, it had been yanked away with the speedboat. I saw its sluggish orange drag through the water as my head cleared when I bobbed up, choking and dog paddling.

"Mommy," I gasped. But the boat was soaring away, building up to full speed, and the occupants too full of exhilaration and the wind in their faces to remember that I existed. The orange life preserver, towed for a few moments, had released from the boat. I could see it, distant and flat. The shore seemed closer, so I began swimming with my ineffective stroke to get to safety.

I paddled till my arms turned to painful sticks and my head, bent back to keep my mouth at the top of the water, ached my neck. I gasped and waved to no one, and lost my balance and sank into the liquid sleeve, my circling feet bringing me back, now more tired than ever. At last it became clear. My struggles were weak, and the shore was too far. I wasn't going to make it. The water was a rubber balloon, bouncing and pushing me off the surface. I sank beneath, and rested with relief. Then I remembered life, and fought back. A breath, tear's wetness that despaired and got lost in the wave, and then it was slow motion, the water now quicksand.

I was under too long, my eyes bugging open, the distance between the top and me impossible, bursting lungs filling with water from my open mouth, and dizziness spearing darkness into my forehead.

I don't remember the moment when he saved me. I awoke to his kiss, as he tried to fill my lungs with air. He had pulled me up into the little boat that he shared with his friend, my ten-year-old weight not hard to bear. The two boys had rowed out to me, but it was him who had jumped in to save me. My eyes opened, but I wasn't restored yet.

"Breathe," he demanded, and I remembered, drawing in air and choking it out again. The oxygen was like electricity, driving me upward and to the side, trying to find a pathway as it pummeled down my veins, changing my bloodstream back to red.

I started coughing and crying.

"All right," he pounded between my shoulder blades. I'd looked up, wiping my eyes and pushing back my hair. And that smile he had for me, his eyes lit with warmth, had burnt his image into my brain.

When we'd gone back home I vowed he'd not be allowed to forget me. I'd trouble him with letters as long as I knew his address. And although I hadn't stopped writing and my letters were sent out with twice-a-month regularity, my most recent letters had changed their tone. I hadn't realized how much until I got his response to my latest yesterday.

Therese, he began, spare as always. *I want to know what's wrong. If you won't write it to me in your letters, then I'll have to come and visit you.*
Miklos

What a thought! Miklos leaving Greece and flying all the way to Seattle to visit me, and just because he suspected something was wrong? He was joking, of course. It seemed impossible. And yet he made it seem so simple.

I'd kept the letter in my pocket since yesterday, and now I pulled it out again. I was sitting by myself in my room. Next door, in the bathroom, I could hear my mother's broken hum as she leaned over the lighted mirror getting ready.

At forty-three my mother was still a force of beauty, for she kept herself bikini-fit. Sit-ups every night, starvation patrols several times a month, the nervous smoking of cigarettes outside on the back porch five times a day. She fussed about her hair, like she was a teenager.

I frowned. In a way, she'd never had the chance to fully grow up. She'd been orphaned at twenty, and pregnant and married by twenty-one. That marriage hadn't lasted very long, and my father had been sent away before he even knew he was to be a father. Her parents had left her a hefty estate, and her needs were simple. She still lived in the same guesthouse, which had been parceled off to her when she sold the fancy house that she grew up in. During the few years of my childhood that she had been married again, we had moved in with my stepfather and then, when the marriage had ended, we had come back here.

But perhaps I wasn't being fair. She had left me alone, and allowed me to do whatever I wanted. She'd listened to me talk, as long as I chose the right time to interrupt her—while she was putting on her makeup or when she was stretched out trying to get a suntan. She hadn't resented me, and in her immature way, she loved me. I was happy enough and relatively safe all the years of my childhood.

But now I spread out Miklos' letter and closed my eyes. What was I going to do? He said he wanted to know what was wrong, but how could I tell him? It was such a stupid problem, and it came right out of a gothic novel.

I heard my mother snap closed her make-up case, indicating that she was satisfied with her appearance. Soon the new man in her life would be arriving. I couldn't help but hesitate. At my age I was able to agree that my mother had a right to be happy. But I wasn't ready for her to get married again, not with my life in its current state of upheaval. And I could tell that this man was determined to take my mother down the aisle, so they could both live a fairy tale romance one more time. He would come in this evening, broad and gregarious and a charming fifty-two. "So how are my girls tonight?" he would boom.

A cheerful knock sounded at the front door, and for a moment I was tempted to gallop out the back.

"Therese, get that, will you?"

"I'm busy."

"I'm not ready yet!" my mother's tone was sharp. One of the rules of our home was never for her to appear before she was ready. I sighed and got up.

I opened the door and the man was leaning against the frame. His hair was graying in all the right places, his complexion was even and brown, but not the brown of Miklos, warm and golden. His frame was sturdy and wide and he carried his middle-aged chest with distinction. He roamed his eyes behind me and to each side.

"Where's your mum, Princess?" he asked. With effort I kept myself from rolling my eyes. I reminded myself that I was not a teenager. I stepped back so he could come in.

"She's getting ready."

"Then we have a few minutes to chat. Why don't you come tell me about your day?"

I remembered that he was a therapist, with a focus on ladies who were dieting. He was very successful, and he was trying to be kind. But I didn't want him to see too much.

"Sorry, I don't have the time," I excused myself. "I need to get ready too."

The man blinked.

"Oh? Got a date?"

"Something like that."

"You should be careful who you go out with, Therese. Some men can't be trusted."

"I'll be careful."

"So tell me about this young man. Where did you meet him?"

He was sounding concerned. His eyes were attentive. When was my mother going to appear?

"I've known him since I was a child," I said. "He's a good friend."

I was eager now to see those two out of the house so I could spend some time writing. Even thousands of miles away, Miklos was a man who could be trusted, even if I didn't tell him everything.

My mother's date nodded and retreated.

"I hope you have a pleasant evening," he said.

I smiled without meeting his eyes. I just wasn't ready for anyone to see me up close.

"I'll go see what's keeping my mother," I replied, backing away.

Chapter Two

"You may have contracted tuberculosis."

That's what the doctor had said to me, two mornings ago. He wanted to do some tests and check my x-rays. I'd been sick for a while, with a persistent cough that kept me up and made me feverish at night. I'd been losing weight too, but so far had managed to hide that fact, as well as the paleness of my face with make-up. Somehow I knew that this was not just a lingering cold or flu. It felt wrong. I was to go back in to see the doctor this morning, and it was easy to get cleaned up and dressed without disturbing my mother.

"This is 1975, not the dark ages," the doctor said to me a short while later. "Using several of the new streptomycins we can treat tuberculosis quite effectively. You'll need to receive a round of injections, the first of which we'll give you today. It's good that you came to be treated so soon, instead of waiting until you were at death's door like a lot of young people do these days. You must rest, no more work. And, once the round of medication is done and you're no longer contagious, it would be good for you to get away to someplace warm, where the air is dry. Perhaps you could go to a desert location. Wouldn't you enjoy that?"

My eyes grew distant even while I coughed as a reaction to his examination. Take a vacation someplace warm? Would I like that?

"Yes, doctor, it would be good to get away," I said. "I know just the place. I have a friend who lives in Crete."

"Then that's what I prescribe," the man responded with a smile. "A month or so in the golden sun of Greece should see your lungs completely healed. But you must rest remember. Not too much exertion."

"Yes, doctor."

I went home and broke the news to my mother. All the news.

"But Therese, you can't go off now, just when Xavier and I were about to ... well, to announce things."

My mother liked me to address her by her first name.

"June, it's not as if I hadn't guessed! You and Xavier make it pretty obvious how you feel about each other. And I won't be leaving for several weeks. I have to be cured of this disease first!"

"Oh, for heaven's sakes don't repeat that to everyone we know! How did you ever come down with tuberculosis, anyway? What my parents used to call 'consumption' isn't it?"

"The doctor said I must have been exposed to it somewhere. While I was working with the volunteer organization, perhaps."

She stopped fussing for a moment and really looked at me. It always spooked me when she did that.

"What are you going to do if you don't recover, Therese?" she asked.

"Die, I suppose."

I saw her shudder, but I didn't know if it was latent mother-love or just a gut reaction to the word "die." But she wasn't done being curious.

"So you want to go to Greece?"

"Yes. I can use that money that's been set aside for me, can't I, June? The money my father used to send twice a year?"

"I always kept that for you. Use it, by all means." She waved an unconcerned hand. But her eyes pierced.

"You're going to see that little boy, aren't you? The one you write to?"

"He's twenty-four now," I reminded her. "All grown up."

"Hmm. A mystery man from Greece. I suppose I should object to you going to him. After all, he may not be such a good fellow now."

"Miklos is a good man," I said, my face indignant. "And I'm not, 'going to him'! I'll find a nice hotel, and just visit him."

She smiled slowly.

"So even you can defend your man like a woman? But I know you won't do anything silly. You've learned that much from me, I hope, Therese. You know I always avoid the bad men."

It was true, and I was grateful. Her need to be adored and sought after never brought home ogres. I softened and smiled, right before going off into a coughing fit.

"Go lie down, pet," she instructed. "I'll talk to Xavier about your trip. He'll take care of everything, and you can relax."

That night I broke my usual routine. I wrote a letter to Miklos, to be posted only two days after my previous letter.

Dear Miklos,

First, I want to thank you for that long and newsy letter you just sent. Two entire sentences is the shortest letter you've ever sent to me. I ask you, have I ever done that to you? Two pages is a small letter for me to send, isn't it? You threaten to come all the way here and visit if I don't tell you everything, and yet, what do you tell me? Nothing but about how your fishing business is going with Andros, or that you bought some new equipment recently?

Well, this letter of mine is to inform you that I've had enough. I'm the one that's been deprived, for YEARS, of finding out what's going on with you. So, if anyone should be visited, it should be you. That's why I'm coming to Crete to visit you instead. It'll take a few weeks for me to resolve a few things, and then I'll come. My mother's new fiancé is going to see to the arrangements and schedule my plane flight and reserve a good room for me to stay in. I'll be flying into Athens, then travel into Crete from there and I'll send you a letter and tell you the details once the arrangements have been made. In the meanwhile, don't worry about what's wrong with me. Coming to Greece will provide the cure.

With affection, Therese

I addressed the envelope and set it on my bedside table. It was a sunny day, for Seattle, pleasant with the flowering trees around the next-door garden at the end of May. I wrapped up in a shawl and went out onto the patio. Finding a spot of sun I pulled out a new book I was reading. Sitting up in the lounge chair instead of lying flat helped me not to cough. Soon I was fast asleep.

The next week or so passed quickly. My mother, energized by my imminent departure, decided to make a complete break and marry her paramour before I left. Feeling unsettled, and unable to resist accompanying her when she begged me to help her select dresses or other items for the wedding, I didn't get quite as much rest as the doctor prescribed. He scolded me during my next visit.

"Now Miss Lindsey, you don't want me to admit you to the hospital, do you?"

"But Doctor, you just said the medicine has taken effect. I should no longer be contagious."

"But your lungs have been damaged, my dear. You need rest to recover."

"I understand. I have been resting, really."

"I want to see you in a few days. Meanwhile, if you haven't stopped losing weight and if you still exhibit symptoms that concern me, I'll put you in the hospital for two weeks."

"Oh, you can't do that. My flight to Greece is in nine days."

"There. I thought that would get your attention."

"I'll do better. I promise."

"See that you do."

I adjusted my clothing and left his office determined to get better. I went home and stayed in bed all evening. But eventually I got hungry, and my mother was on starvation patrol due to the fact that she wanted to look splendid on her upcoming honeymoon. In the kitchen while I opened a can of Campbell's chicken noodle soup, she wandered in. I stopped stirring to look at her.

She seemed happy, her eyes dreamy and distracted. Something inside my chest relaxed. Maybe she was going to be all right. Maybe Xavier really was all that he seemed to be. At any rate, my mother was an adult, and it was her life. It was time for me to give her my best send off and get on with mine.

"I'm going to eat soup and then stay in bed tonight, June," I told her. "The doctor threatened me with a hospital stay if I didn't start getting better sooner, and I don't want to miss my flight to Greece."

She stopped puttering and really looked me in the eye like she had the other day. Woman to woman, we understood each other, for once. We were each involved in our own adventures. And yet, there was more between us. We were more than parent and child, and more than friends. In our independent ways, we had been all in all to each other, but now all that was about to change. She blinked, and a mist appeared for a split second in her flawless painted eyes.

"I understand, Therese," she said. "Go get some rest. I'll take care of my own business."

"Thank you, Mother," I slipped in, because I couldn't help it. A flash of humor replaced the sentiment on her face. She would allow the title, this time, but her expression told me not to make a habit of it. When I went in to my room, with my dinner on a tray and some glossy magazines next to the piled pillows on my bed I snuggled in like a burrowing hamster.

My mother asked no more favors, and allowed Xavier to step in and attend to details. He was very good at it. Furniture movers came and took away the few pieces my mother desired to adorn his very nice Edwardian cottage with. Gardeners put the lawn and the trees to rest. Arrangers and cake decorators paid calls to my mother and defined her wishes into a hurried, elegant and expensive last-minute wedding.

I was maid of honor, and my mother's three best friends from her girlhood stood in a line next to me.

When the organ played and my mother moved by herself down the aisle, resplendent in an off-white, lace edged suit that showed her elegant legs below the knee, I admired her as she marched toward us. The high-heeled shoes matched the color of the suit with perfection. Her hat nestled in her styled blond curls. She was trim and beautiful and I was proud of her. And when I saw her dancing eyes and the irrepressible soul of the teenager that still lived inside her, I wished fervently for her to be happy.

They were married by noon, and the reception ended at two o'clock. My new stepfather had pulled me aside that morning and admonished me to let the wedding planners attend to the clean up, and reminded me of where he had placed my tickets and instructions to go to Greece. My mother had slipped in and told me to be careful and write to her often; giving me their honeymoon itinerary and the addresses of all the hotels they would be staying in. After the reception I was driven home in the taxi my stepfather had arranged.

I wandered around my empty house with a sigh, once I was alone and the celebrating was done. I stretched my weary shoulders, and coughed in a weak way, for old time's sake. The doctor's threats had never materialized, even though I wasn't as strong as he liked. But he agreed I could go. I wasn't going to infect anyone, and he hoped that while I was in Greece and the golden warm sun, that I would get better at last.

Picking up a pile of Miklos' letters I stuffed them in my suitcase. I hadn't told him what was wrong with me yet, but soon he would know all about me. I wondered what he would think of me. But I was committed now. And if he didn't like me, and our friendship turned out to be based on nothing, then it was time I realized it and quit holding him up as such an ideal. Either way, Greece was sure to be the launching point to my new life. I clicked my suitcase closed with a snap that reminded me of my mother and her make-up case. I was satisfied with my preparations.

Chapter Three

It was strange on the day of my departure to have no one say goodbye to me at the airport. But with my stepfather's detailed instructions I navigated the taxi ride and the baggage check-in with ease. I waited in the terminal, awed by the towering windows of the Seattle-Tacoma Airport. It wasn't until I was on the last connection, the plane flying into the airport in Greece, that I realized I recognized one of the passengers.

It wasn't a pleasant association. A few weeks ago after my diagnosis, I had sat in a stark examination room waiting for the technician to come in and give me another round of chest x-rays. Instead this man had come in.

Such a strange feeling had enveloped me when my small room had been invaded. This man wasn't wearing a lab coat. He wasn't carrying a clipboard. He didn't give me an impersonal smile that set me at professional ease. And, he didn't say a single word. He just entered and shut the door behind him, and glared at me with fixation. I asked him if there was something he wanted, but he didn't reply. Right when I began to fear for my safety he finished examining my features and left. The technician came in two minutes later and gave me the impersonal smile I was expecting.

I stared at the man now, where he sat on the plane two rows up from me. He was distinctive looking and I was surprised that I hadn't realized sooner. He had a massive bulk of shoulder that must have required that his tan sports jacket be custom made. He looked like some henchman out of a comic book, for he had short stubby blond hair, several lines of scars across chin and cheek, and those empty eyes.

I took a deep breath and chided myself for being fanciful. Yes, there was no doubt that it was the same man, but his being on my plane had nothing to do with me. It was just an odd coincidence.

I picked up my magazine, the May 1975 issue of Vogue, and tried to forget the man. The magazine's cover featured a blue-eyed model, wearing a blue swimsuit, a powder blue phone to her ear and the brilliant blue that denoted sun and surf behind her. Just looking at it made me feel warm all over, knowing that soon I was going to end up in an island of Greece; there to sit on the rock-dusted sand, staring at blue water that came out of the sunlight's paint box. I closed my eyes and remembered the light of Crete. Like nowhere else I'd ever seen. Even though I had been a child when I last saw it, I knew that this wouldn't disappoint me.

When the plane set down in Athens at last and was disembarking, the man I was avoiding sat in his seat and let the other passengers go, until the moment that I collected up my bag and my sunglasses. I squeezed by him, for a plump woman was on the other side of the aisle fussing with a flowered hat that she was determined to arrange on her hair without the aid of a mirror.

"Excuse me," I said, taking in a breath of perfume. I had to touch the man's legs as I passed, and I was unsettled to feel his muscles move, for he rose to leave at that moment, slipping in to be the one that exited the plane directly behind me.

Athens Airport was lost on me. I was too busy looking through the crowds for a familiar face, and trying to forget the scarred face of the man behind me. Miklos had gotten the letter I sent with my arrangements, and had written a reply promising to meet me when I arrived.

Soon I noticed someone standing still a few feet away, and the crowds cleared the space in between us at the same time that I looked up and saw my name handwritten on a paper sign. The next thing I saw was a huge, joyful grin. Miklos didn't look like he had when he was twelve. He was about five-foot-nine, built slender but stocky in the shoulders. His hair was multi-colored and tousled, with sandy-brown edges. There were creases beside his smile, and there was a long straight nose. Recognition came when I met his eyes. He wasn't handsome like movie stars were handsome. But he was my friend, unchanged, buoyant and before me at last in grasping range. The weary shell of my shoulders relaxed. My response grew from down deep, and demanded that my return smile fill my face as his was doing. I set down my bags and came up to him, welcoming the awkward moment of first touch. I held out both hands and he took them, to be courteous. But when that gesture was satisfied he laughed and pulled me into a hearty embrace. He pounded the space between my shoulder blades, and the wretched cough, nearly forgotten over the last few days, sprang forth at the very moment when I least wanted it.

When I was done and lifted my handkerchief and apologetic eyes, his hand was still on my shoulder and he looked thoughtful.

"Excuse me, Miklos. I'm so excited to see you after all these years."

"You don't seem much larger than you did at ten-years-old, little Pouli," he replied, in his accent-tilted English. But he spoke fluid and well.

"Little Pouli? What does that mean?"

"Pouli is a bird. Here, you must let me take those."

He reached down for my suitcases.

"I don't look like a bird!"

He laughed.

"We can't have an argument first thing," he said.

"But Miklos, you shouldn't have come to meet me here in Athens! You should have waited for a few days for me to fly into Crete! What will you do till then?"

"The man who made the arrangements for you wanted you to sightsee here in Athens for a nice holiday, yes? Well I know Athens quite well! I'll show you all the best spots! I have friends who live here, and I'll stay with them. And, tonight you'll go with me to meet them. You'll love the food."

"But don't you have to work?"

"Work? While my very own friend has flown all the way from America? You have much to discover about me, don't you? Many questions to ask?"

"I can see that you've been holding in all the words you didn't send me in your letters all these years," I teased. "You'll wash me away like a wave on the shore!"

"And you'll be silent then, eh, Pouli? We'll switch places?"

"Stop sounding so hopeful. I'm a woman, not a bird."

All this while we had been walking outside into the Athens sunshine, past the drive in front of the airport where the taxis sat, and at last we came to a stop in front of a dusty pale blue Austin

1800. He opened the trunk for my suitcases and grinned.

"And a bird must sing, is that what you're saying?"

I shook my head, accepting the inevitable. And, to tell the truth, I didn't mind my new nickname.

"Just for that I'll bend your ear until we reach my hotel," I warned him.

"'Bend my ear?'"

"An American colloquialism."

"Ah," he said. "Slang."

He opened the passenger door with a flourish and helped me inside. I wondered whose car this was, and why I felt so comfortable with him. But just as he shut the door with a bang and trotted around to the driver's side of the car I sat far back in my seat, unsettled. That strange man from the plane had followed us to the pavement. He was standing within touching distance, staring with fixation at Miklos, the little car, and me. But he said nothing. I shuddered and looked back as the car roared to life and leapt into the lane, not able to help myself. The blond man climbed into a taxi and I saw his mouth move as he gave his direction to the driver. I turned forward and clenched my hands around my bag. I suspected that the fellow behind us was going to follow our car all the way to my hotel.

"Everything all right, Therese?" Miklos said. "You look scared all of a sudden! Have you decided that my driving is that bad already?"

I glanced to the back of us again.

"Perhaps you could go faster then?" I said without thinking.

"Faster!"

I blinked and met his eye.

"There's someone behind …"

I didn't finish the sentence. He was watching me close, and I took in the clear brown of his eyes. He had good lashes, I thought. He swerved, driving by feel.

"At least glance at the road every so often," I urged.

He nodded and laughed, turning to the front to see the road so he could pick up speed.

"I knew you couldn't resist scolding me!" he boomed, triumphant.

I fell into satisfied silence after that, watching the window now for a close up view of Athens as we approached it. The airport was a few miles out, and I admired the wooded hills and scattered white residences nearby. Miklos let the silence fall, concentrating on his driving, and yet his face was relaxed and pleased with my company. I felt glad to know that we could be quiet together without awkwardness. I let peace lean me back in my seat, my eyes dreamy as Athens finally began to surround us. It was a bustling city, its streets filled with tourist-related small businesses and uneven squares of concrete and old stone, knee-high walls. Stairs were carved everywhere, sometimes in a narrow space between two buildings, and sometimes up a hill to more beautiful architecture. And behind it all, green hills lush with vegetation, glimpses of the ancient, until at last he turned a corner and I saw the best view of the Acropolis I had seen yet settled majestically on a hill.

How comfortable the ruins sat here in the city. As if she were an old patient grandmother sitting watch in the sunshine, shaking her head at all the little buildings that comprised her children and great-great-grandchildren. I grinned at Miklos and got my arm out the window, waving an excited hand of greeting at my first glimpse of the Parthenon. Beside me Miklos was caught up in my enthusiasm. As we both laughed I forgot all about the stubby-haired blond man, and any possibility of pursuit.

Chapter Four

The hotel he took me to was called the Hotel Adrian, and was located in a wonderful part of Athens called the Plaka district. I could see the Acropolis from some of its windows. My room was on the top floor, and I stepped out onto my little balcony. A wrought iron table with a flowering plant invited me to sit outside and absorb the warmth of sun and the color of the life bustling in the romantic little streets. I went back into the room and sat on the twin bed, smiling to myself when Miklos banged the doorway with my suitcases and muttered something that sounded rich and melodious under his breath.

"I could have helped you with those cases, you know," I commented. "You didn't even let me carry my bag."

"You looked like a pouli with broken wings under these cases," he returned. "What have you put in them, American bricks of stone?"

He set the cases down in the open closet space.

"I put all the things that young ladies require for comfort and pleasing the eye in them, of course."

He stared down at me and smiled.

"Then it's worth it," he said. "You look charming, although spindly."

"Spindly?"

"A good English word, isn't it? You used it in one of your letters."

"I see that my letters have increased your English vocabulary."

"In order to understand your letters for myself, I had to take night classes. I went ahead and got a degree while I was at it, in business with a side degree in the English language."

"You did? I'm so sorry I didn't learn Greek too. That wasn't fair of me, Miklos."

"You can learn it while you're here! Aren't you going to stay for two months?"

"That's a tall order. I haven't the least idea of what that little sign says out in the hall or how to read a street sign! Your Greek letters are very pretty, but incomprehensible."

I yawned.

"You're tired," he said.

"A little. It was a long journey."

"You're pale," he added.

I felt a little self-conscious.

"Seattle isn't known for its sunny days."

"Are you ready now to tell me what's wrong?"

I looked away, not wanting to hide things, but unwilling to face the possibility that tuberculosis might scare him away.

"I've been ... unwell," I said at last.

His face flooded with dismay. He sat right next to me, crowding the narrow bed.

"Unwell? Are you sick, Therese?"

"Yes, but I'm getting better. The doctor said I needed to go someplace warm so I could recover."

"And did the doctor say what was causing your illness?"

"Yes, but I'm afraid to tell you."

"Afraid! Do you think I will be angry?"

"No, but I think you might ..."

I bit my lip, and his face formed the first frown I had seen from him.

"You think I might be ashamed of you, Pouli? Do you think I'm the sort of friend who pulls away when needed the most?"

"Now you look angry. I don't mean to offend you."

"Then begin this conversation again. What is wrong? I've been worried for months. I knew that something had changed with you. Your letters lost their ..." He paused for the right word. "... life," he finished.

I stared at him closely, at the uptilted corners of his lips, the sturdy line of his jaw, and his eyes, which I decided now were beautiful. My heart began thumping. But I could see that I had no choice. If I didn't tell him, his feelings would be hurt, and I couldn't do that to him, no matter if he changed toward me.

"I went down to the south end of my country a while ago. There was some volunteer work I went to do. Right on the border, I went with a group of young people to help build a small school for a poor community. We crossed the border often, while we were there, and I made friends with a few children from Mexico. One of them was sick, but I didn't think much of it at the time. I picked it up from her. I only hope that she recovered, but I have no way of contacting her to find out."

He reached over and took my two hands, like we had done when we met at the airport. He waited.

"Tuberculosis," I supplied at last.

By instinct I pulled my hands, expecting him to recoil. But he squeezed until I stopped.

"Uh... you're grip is very strong ..."

"I'm sorry, Therese. This shouldn't have happened to you! I see now all the signs! And the way you coughed in the airport!"

"Don't worry, Miklos. The doctor assured me that I'm no longer contagious."

"Do you think that's what I'm upset about?"

"I've taken a lot of injections, strong antibiotics."

"And now you'll rest. I'll go away for a few hours, yes?" He got up and plumped my pillows.

"It feels strange to have a man in my room arranging my bed," I said, my voice dry.

He reared up and dropped the pillow. I saw his cheeks go red.

"Of course, a young lady would find that uncomfortable! Of course I didn't mean to frighten you! I wasn't ..."

I laughed.

"You're cute when you're flustered," I told him.

He blinked and I watched the corner of his mouth as he lifted it. He came forward and took hold of my shoulders and looked down into my eyes.

"And you," he breathed, "are a skinny bird."

I shoved him away, affronted.

"Oh, go away, for a while!"

Peace was restored and he stepped to the door.

"I'll come back in three hours," he said. "Look at your little watch. It'll be evening, and we'll go and meet my friends for dinner."

"I'm looking forward to meeting your friends. Thank you for

coming for me at the airport, Miklos. I admit I would've been confused trying to find my way."

"Then don't wander the streets by yourself. Let me show you how first, all right?"

"I'll stay right here."

"And sleep?"

"I'll take a nap and then get ready."

"Good girl."

This time he came up and kissed my forehead before going out.

•

Two and-a-half hours later I woke up from my nap, stretched out my arms luxuriously in the twin bed, and screamed.

That man, the one from the hospital examination room and the plane, was a mere two feet from my face. He was bending over me, staring again with no expression, as if he were some sort of robot soldier from Planet Nine. His yellow, stubby hair looked sharp like the beard bristle that was visible up close.

"What do you want?" my voice was shrill, but as he made no movement, I allowed my thoughts to plan escape. I slid sideways out from under him and got to my feet. At the door I snatched my purse, and seeing him turn to follow I slammed the door shut in his face. I ran down the hallway, hearing my door open after him.

Down the stairs, bursting out the door of the hotel into the sunshine, I kept on running, glancing back and seeing him in pursuit.

It wasn't long before I realized that I had forgotten my shoes. I turned and ran up some steps, drawn to a picturesque little stone alley with a slant of late afternoon sunshine illuminating one wall in bold diagonal stripes.

In front of me on the other side the view opened to a stone lawn, variegated by a turquoise blue wall, a painted ocher chair, and a splash of fuchsia-colored flowers along a pure white windowsill. I pushed through a narrow pathway of whitewashed walls.

Panting now, my feet learning Athens by feel, the world of sound cascaded around me, almost forgotten from my quiet room and the peaceful yet deserted courtyards I had just passed through. Cars were crowding, inventing lanes and pathways in the street ahead of me. The taxis were all a blue-gray color, and there were several that passed in haphazard speed.

I began walking in a brisk trot, pretending as I joined the strolling crowd on the sidewalk that I was a normal tourist, albeit barefoot. But soon I was trotting, adrenalin urging me to run in out and out of streets and flat rock-floored hide-a-ways. Up one street, slipping with cleverness down a side alley, and clutching my purse to my chest, I slowed at the end of a road with more stone palisades. Here it was empty once more, and I craved a moment alone. Seeing a low cement wall I went and sat against it, bending forward and wiping my eyes.

A coughing fit attacked and I choked, trying to catch my breath. My fingers were trembling and not just because I had been scared in my room. I wasn't well, and hadn't been for weeks. I wasn't up to running full tilt through the heat of a Grecian sun. But at least I was certain that the strange man was no longer following me. Getting a hold of myself I thought that he hadn't been chasing me for some while. And it made sense. A pale American woman, running down the street barefoot and looking wild, might cause comment. But a muscular, soulless-looking man chasing her would have to be dealt with by any passerby with a sense of decency.

I began to feel a little better and I stood straight, running my fingers through my long, auburn-brown hair, poofing my bangs. My simple, rounded-collar, pink and orange sun dress looked fine, and I pulled at a few wrinkles till the hem rested at a sedate six inches above my knee. As I draped my purse over my shoulder and prepared to mingle in public again, I missed my white, lace-up, knee-high boots that I'd left in my room, as well as the swirl hair scarf of matching colors that I accessorized with when I wore this dress. I wasn't a trendy, young girl of the seventies right now, but a distressed, confused stranger to beautiful Athens.

I went back a half a block and reemerged into the bustle of the busy street. Then I came to a stop. I had no idea how to get back to my hotel. I was lost in a city where I could read no signs, among people who spoke a different language. What was I going to do?

Chapter Five

Of course one isn't in real trouble in the daylight streets of Athens. I merely had to look around, choose a shopkeeper who looked accommodating, and go up to him and tell him my problem. He had some English, enough to understand that I wanted to return to Hotel Adrian.

He gave me directions, and was so eager to help that I pretended to understand them. I thanked him and was warmed by his effusive good will. I went two blocks in the right direction, and found another shopkeeper to ask. This one was in a bookstore, and the rows of books, some of them in English, almost tempted me to browse. But Miklos was due to arrive soon, if he wasn't at my hotel already.

"Hotel Adrian?" I asked, and the man picked up what I wanted fast. Soon we were standing in the street and I had more directions to follow.

Two shopkeepers later I was able to recognize the street I was on, and soon with relief I hurried into my hotel. Anxiety returned once I left the lobby and entered the deserted stairwell. Silence coated the hallway up to my door. Was the man with the stubby hair still hiding in my room? My weariness returned at the thought.

I stopped a few feet from my door and listened. I heard nothing, no sounds of movement, not even from the street outside. Taking my courage in hand I went to my door, opened it, and peeked inside. No one.

I wondered as I ventured in and examined every corner of room and balcony if I wanted to continue to stay here. I had liked the funny little hotel right away and it would be a shame to leave. I saw that my suitcases were open, and some of my things were spilling out. My pillow and blankets had been pulled off the bed in my wild flight. Even a rickety table that had held a small vase and a writing pad by the door was knocked over.

I didn't like the thought that the man had gone through my suitcases. But after all, I had taken my purse with me, with all of my relevant identification and my wallet inside. Only my clothes and my toiletries were to be found in my cases, and those, if necessary, could be replaced. Except for ... dismay filled me as I fell to my knees beside the cases and pawed through the spilled contents.

My letters! The letters from Miklos that I had saved all these years! I hadn't brought them all, but a sampling of my favorites, which I had planned to show to him and laugh over when we had some time alone. It didn't take long to make certain. The letters were gone. That awful man had stolen them. If he had held me at knifepoint and demanded my most precious valuables he couldn't have hurt me more.

It all caught up to me then. The changes in my life, and the virtual loss of my mother, the illness that made catching my breath during any emergency draining, the recent fright and the sense of violation, but most of all that some cold man had taken my letters. I sat flat on my knees with my legs splayed, put my face in my hands and cried.

That's how he discovered me. Miklos pulled wide my open door and hurried in, words spilling out.

"There you are, Therese. When I came to get you and found your door open, and your room a mess! I was worried, but all the man behind the counter in the lobby could tell me was ..."

He noticed that I wasn't getting up.

"You're crying," he spouted. He got down to my level, and patted my shoulder. "Are you all right? What happened? Are you hurt, or sick?"

His agitated voice broke through, and I sniffed and swiped at my eyes.

"I'm all right," I managed.

"But what has happened?"

My jaw started trembling in spite of my efforts. "He took my letters!"

"What letters? Who did it?

"The letters you wrote me, Miklos! I've kept them all these

years, and I wanted to show them to you."

He stared at me for a few seconds, but the only thing to see was that I started crying again. So he got up, grasping my shoulders and raising me with him. He led me over to sit on my bed. Shutting my door with a glance outside he stepped into the tiny bathroom and ran the sink for a minute. Then he came out with a damp washcloth and patted my face with it.

"Shh," he soothed, saying nothing. His ministrations made me want to cry more, to release the doors of emotion. But I was an adult and not a child. In a few seconds I had regained my composure.

"I'm sorry," I whispered.

"No, no," he said.

"I'm better now."

"Good."

"It's just that your letters mean a lot to me, Miklos."

"Don't start crying again."

"I know its silly, but I've kept them and reread them and ..."

"It is silly. My letters aren't worth seeing you cry. I'll write you more letters. A hundred letters."

That made me smile.

"You sound like you're talking to a five-year-old."

"I can think of nothing to say to that which won't get me into trouble."

"You can deny it, you cad."

"Ah ha! I know what cad means. And would a cad sit here like this?"

"I suppose not. I haven't been much fun for you so far, I guess, and I wanted to make this visit fun for you."

"There's more to being a friend than just having fun."

I sighed and sat up straight.

"Therese, I have questions," he reminded me.

I nodded. Of course he did, and so did I. The trouble was, I had no answers. That man took Miklos's letters, and it was easy to guess why. Two reasons came to my mind: one, so he could read the words and find out what sort of person Miklos was; and two, so he could have Miklos's address.

That bothered me a great deal. It didn't seem to matter where I stayed in Athens, or if I tried to be sneaky and hide from my assailant; because he knew where I was going. Or at least, he could locate my friend at his address in Crete and bother him or follow him until he led him to me.

"I'm so sorry, Miklos. He took your letters, and now he has your address."

"Who did?"

"That man."

"What man?"

"The one who ..."

"Don't stop there. Tell me what man is this? Do you have some angry boyfriend, Therese? Has he followed you here to Greece?"

"Oh no, nothing like that. I don't know who this man is."

"Then how do you know it was a man who took the letters? Perhaps it was a woman, a maid even? Or perhaps you lost them?"

"But he was here, in my room. And on the plane, and at the airport. And in my examination room back in Seattle."

"Tell me everything. Start at the beginning."

I gathered my thoughts together.

"At the hospital back home the doctor told me I was sick. He told me I had tuberculosis and it was a rare case, that some other doctors might stop in to see me. I was alone in an examination room, waiting for an attendant to talk to me about some tests. And this man came in. At first I thought little of it. But he didn't speak to me; he just stared, until I began to get concerned. Then he left and I forgot about him."

"And this was ..."

"A few weeks ago, I'm not sure when. And then I saw him on the plane, right as we were about to land in Athens."

"And you're sure it was the same man?"

"He's very distinctive looking. I thought perhaps I was mistaken as well. But then he followed me out of the airplane, and he stood beside us when you packed your car at the airport. He stared at us, and your car."

"Why didn't you say something?"

"Because it was so odd! I thought for sure that he was just peculiar, that perhaps he remembered seeing me before and wanted an eyeful again."

"Wanted an eyeful?"

"You understand what I mean, right?"

A small smile.

"Yes, I'll remember that one. Go on."

"Then when I woke up from my nap, a little while ago here in my room, he was bending over me."

"He had followed you here, and was in this room? Are you sure?"

"Of course I'm sure. He saw me scream and ignored my questions. He did nothing as I pulled away from him and got to the door. He followed me outside but didn't chase me when I ran. I ran too far and got lost. By the time I made my way back here he was gone, with my letters."

"And you don't know why he keeps appearing? He never said one word to you?"

"Not one."

He stared into space and then frowned.

"I don't like that he came right into your room while you were sleeping," he growled. "So don't worry. We'll call the police."

By the time the police came I had my room put back into order and my bed was tidy. I had my boots on and my hair pulled back into a thick ponytail at the nape of my neck with the scarf tied around it.

Miklos helped with the translation; although the policeman had a good grasp of English, it was easy to see that my friend had more.

But, there was nothing much that the policeman could do for me. I didn't know who the stubby-haired man was, after all. Once the report had been taken Miklos asked if I felt well enough to go visit his friends.

"It's very late for dinner," I replied with a smile.

"They will have saved dinner for us," he assured me.

"Well then we can't disappoint them."

His friends were a young married couple, newlyweds a few years older than me, but the dinner was served at the wife's parent's house. There were younger siblings, a few cousins, and I could see that Miklos was considered a member of the family. I was greeted with welcome, the young woman from America that he wrote letters with. During the meal the young wife came and sat by me, beginning a conversation.

"My name is Accalia," she reminded me.

"I'm Therese."

"Yes, I know," she said in a heavy accent. "Miklos has spoken of you often. He's very proud that you wanted to be his friend when you were children."

"Well, I suppose all little girls would want to be the friend of the boy that saved their life," I grinned. Accalia said nothing, but her eyes spoke volumes. I liked this Greek girl. She seemed willing to step beyond the face of courtesy, and show me real sarcasm. In fact, she was only two years older than me, like Miklos.

"What?" I demanded with a laugh. "Why are you smiling at me like that?"

"He saved your life when you were children," she said. "It's romantic, no?"

I held up my hands.

"I was ten."

"But you're not ten now."

I grinned.

"And Miklos is no longer twelve," I added, my voice just as arch. And then we both laughed.

"Let's talk of other things," she invited. "For instance, I love those boots of yours. Tell me where you got them?"

Thus began a conversation in which both of us delighted. An hour later, as I glanced at the darkness outside the small windows of the pleasant home, I realized that it was my first night in Athens. When Miklos and I stepped out into the moonlight, I wished my new friends goodnight. She had her arm hooked in mine, and Miklos and her husband, who was named Georgi, were talking to each other a few feet away.

"But I'll see you soon," Accalia said to me. "Miklos is taking you right now to our apartment."

I blinked in surprise.

"What?"

Her husband stepped forward to second the invitation.

"Miklos pointed out that you're not a tourist, with no friends in Greece. Your first night here you must feel like you're visiting family."

I protested, but they were going to be hurt if I didn't accept. Once I got in the car and Miklos began driving I shrank against my seat and watched him. We were alone together for the first time since night fell.

"Don't look at me like that, little Pouli," he said after a moment.

"Miklos, did you tell them everything?"

"Not at all! But I don't like the idea of you staying alone in that hotel room at night."

"So you took over and made new arrangements for me? Without even asking me what I preferred? I'm not a girl from Greece, you know. I'm used to my independence."

A crease settled over his brows.

"It wasn't like that, Therese."

"Then how was it? 'Oh, you must help my poor little American friend? She's sick and helpless and pathetic'?"

He swerved, cutting off a speedy taxi behind us that had just made a move to invent a lane beside us. The taxi's horn blared in my ears. Then he angled right over and pulled to an abrupt stop against a broken stone curb.

"Therese, I don't think of you like that."

"Then what?"

"You just don't understand Greek hospitality. I merely began asking my friends about the idea, in case I could talk to you later, and they took my words and ..."

He sought for the right description to use, and muttered in Greek.

"They took your words and ran off with them?" I couldn't help but supply. His face broke out into a bountiful grin.

"Yes, they ran off with me!" he agreed.

I shook my head, unable to do anything but forgive him. And he took up my hands for the third time that day.

"It's not for you that I asked my friends," he said. "But for me. So I won't worry. Tomorrow, I'll bring you back to your room and you can gather your things. We'll find another hotel for you to stay in."

I didn't have the strength to remind him that the nameless man had taken my letters and therefore had his address. It was better for Miklos to be free of worry as much as possible. But as I acquiesced and looked out the windows at Athens lit up at night, I wondered what it could mean. Why had that man come to my room? What did he want? A few minutes later Miklos pulled up in front of a tall wall of windows and little balconies in an apartment complex. Soon he had left me at the door, with Accalia pulling me in and promising me the best of one of her nightgowns.

The couch was already made up with a thin blanket over the sheets and a simple pillow. It was late, and I yawned saying goodnight to Miklos. It had been a long day.

Chapter Six

I woke up the next morning to see Georgi pulling on his coat to go to work, and Accalia leaning up to kiss him. My face against the pillow I smiled, for they were a beautiful couple. They never noticed me as he left, and I watched their silhouettes through half-closed eyes; her slender arm handing him his lunch, his stronger arm around her waist. He stroked her cheek and once the door closed behind him she hugged herself with a bemused expression. I closed my eyes. It wasn't a moment meant for me. When I opened them again she was gone, disappeared back into her room.

I tried to be quiet as I got up and visited their bathroom, figuring out the unusual shower fixtures, realizing once I was finished that I didn't have my clothes with me. There was a robe hung on the door, and I slipped into it. I grinned as it came down low and sagged with extra material. It was Georgi's. With caution I opened the door and peeked out, hearing sounds in the kitchen. But it was only Accalia, and she turned and leaned back against her counter and smiled at me.

"You look charming in Georgi's clothes," she said.

"Will he mind, do you think?"

"He will never know it. Do you think I want my husband to think of how some other woman looks wearing his robe?"

"I don't think I'm any threat. You're the only woman in his mind."

She looked satisfied, and I thought how pretty she was, with her wavy hair disheveled into curls and the way she owned the morning. She stood straight and came up and measured our heights as we stood nose to nose.

"But we must find you something to wear," she said. "You're

only a little taller than me, Therese. Come on."

We went into her room, where she opened wide her closet. She pulled out only the best for me to try on, and it was a good long time before we were both satisfied. Her clothes fit me well, and I settled on a powder blue dress, with a print of fluttering birds, that was simple and yet with the matching belt brought out my waist. I insisted on giving her my dress in return, getting by her objections by saying that the trade made us family. She looked adorable in my dress, using the scarf as a band to hold back her curls. We were still involved in lively conversation about clothes and accessories, in which the language differences made us both laugh a lot, when a knock came at the door. She was very comfortable with English, but again, she didn't know as much as Miklos.

We were casual as we wandered out to the main room. We were sure that it was Miklos now, coming as he said he would to take me sight seeing. The knock was repeated and she opened the door, finishing a funny story she was telling me. But as I looked up the light died out of my eyes. It wasn't Miklos standing there. It was him, that strange man.

He'd somehow found me, tracked me down until I was at this innocent girl's apartment, my new friend with her generosity and her kindness and her handsome young husband leaving her in safety to go off to work. I pushed her back without thinking and tried to slam closed the door. He wedged in a knee.

"Therese," Accalia was saying, but he had taken hold of my arms before I had even let go of the door.

"What do you want? Why are you here?"

He didn't answer me. He pulled me through the gap, and slammed the door shut on Accalia's startled face. Then he took my shoulders and shook me, hard. My neck strained and my hair flew. I cried, and choked, gasped and rejected air. The cough came forth, ripped sideways out of my mouth, jagged and throaty and seizing my breath. I sucked in noisily, but now he stepped back, ignoring Accalia, who had reappeared. He watched me cough, bent over and traumatized. And then, without looking back, he turned and walked away. Accalia came out and tugged at me, saying many things in her agitation. I didn't answer her questions, for I was trying to put my chest back together, folding the cough away into the closets, covering my mouth with the back of my hand.

We went into her apartment and she closed and locked the door. I was feeling better now that the threat had left, and I pushed back my hair, sitting with shaky limbs on the couch. She was talking in Greek, very fast.

"I'm sorry, Accalia!" I gasped.

She went on talking very fast, coming up and sitting by me.

"Are you all right?" she demanded.

"Yes, I'm fine."

"That terrible man! I can't believe that some stranger would do such a thing!"

"It is terrible," I cried, not knowing where to go from there. But before we could tell each other anything more a sharp sound made us both jump, and my heart hit against the inner wall of my rib cage. It was another knock at the front door.

My hands whipped to my cheeks, and so did hers.

"Oh no!"

"What should we do?"

"Maybe we should run out! Is there a back door we could use?"

A second knock sounded and we both, without making any plan beforehand, screamed. After that, the doorknob rattled, and we shrieked again.

"Therese!" someone called through the door. "Accalia! Are you two all right? Why are you screaming?"

We both sagged in relief. It was Miklos, his warm voice reassuring. It was a few seconds before we could answer.

"Girls!" he yelled, his voice tinged with urgency. The door was shaking now, back and forth as he tried to force it.

"Stop!" Accalia called, getting up. She said a few sentences in Greek to him as she unlocked the door. Then it was open, and he stood there, taking in the scene, and our two faces.

"No," was all he said, before he mumbled something low in his throat that could only be a swear word.

"It was that man again, Miklos."

"Where?"

"Here! He just left!"

Miklos surprised me. He turned, slammed by the front doorframe, and ran down the apartment hallway. I stared for a moment, and then, realizing that I should own this problem instead of all my friends, I scurried after him.

I heard Accalia protest behind me. The hallway stretched ahead, and I saw Miklos disappear down the stairwell. I'd never catch up to him at this rate. But I didn't need to worry. By the time I got halfway down the stairs he was coming back. He lifted his head and trotted up the stairs between us, holding my eyes. We both slowed at the contact, until I was standing still and he was approaching one step at a time.

Greek courtesy, the endless welcoming charm toward friends, its barrier was gone. His face was real now, serious, angry, and sparking with intelligence. Miklos was more than I had realized, and more than he'd let me know. His letters had been mere responses to my girlish growing up, while he had constructed a successful business, completed a degree in night school, and cultivated many friends on his Island of Crete, and even here. He reached me and I was trembling, but no longer because of my assailant. It was him who affected me now, those eyes of his, and the desire to run my fingers through his hair. My hands rose to my cheeks again, and they felt hot.

"It's all right, Pouli," he said, one strong hand on my shoulder. "He's gone."

I got a hold of myself. What had I been thinking? This was Miklos, a man I barely knew by sight, and yet I knew deeply from my thought of him through the years. And yet he was still a stranger to me, and a kind person who didn't deserve to be dragged into whatever was going on.

"I need to get away from here," I said, to him or myself I wasn't sure. "It's not fair to Accalia and Georgi."

"I'll take you," he stated, "wherever you want to go."

"I should get away from you, too."

His eyes narrowed.

"You don't deserve this," I added.

He blinked.

"This isn't something you should have to deal with," I asserted.

"And so I should do what?" he said at last. "Take you back to your hotel and leave you? Go on back to my home and wonder for the rest of my life what happened to you after I deserted you?"

"Don't be melodramatic."

"Whatever that means, I don't like it."

"Well I should leave you, Miklos. Were the situation reversed, you'd think the same thing."

He muttered, and the sentence was a long one.

"Quit swearing at me in Greek."

"Shall I translate it into English?"

"Yes."

He smiled.

"I don't think that should be your first lesson in my language."

I chuckled too.

"Come on," I said. "Accalia must be wondering. I don't know what to tell her."

"The same thing you'll tell me. Everything about this man, and what it is you think can be going on."

He went up the stair above me, and took my elbow in his firm grasp. We went back down the hallway to Accalia, who was on the phone. She was talking in an agitated voice, and I wondered whom it was that she had called first; her husband or her parents or her best friend? I felt bad to have brought this to her home. She met our eyes as we came in and waved us to sit on her couch. She reported to the person on the other end of the line that she needed to say goodbye, and then she hung up. She tilted her head at the salient looks on our faces. We all sat and stared at each other and I sighed.

"I don't know who that man is," I spouted. "I don't know what he wants,"

"What happened just now?" Miklos asked. "What did he say?"

"He said nothing. He knocked at the door and we answered it, thinking it was you. He pulled me out into the hallway and shook me."

"He shook you?"

"Yes."

"Are you all right?"

I rubbed the back of my neck.

"Yes. He left after that."

Miklos leaned forward, his elbows on his knees. He sent the direct look over to his friend.

"Accalia?"

"Yes," she agreed. "That's what happened. He shook her, very rough, and left." She changed partners. "You mean you know who this man is, Therese? You've seen him before?"

I filled her in on what I knew, and apologized once more.

"No, no," she said.

I wondered how far Greek courtesy extended. But I wasn't going to press and find out. I stood up.

"I'd say I was worried about leaving you here alone, Accalia, but I think you'll be a lot safer if I leave," I said.

"My brother's on the way over here now," she replied. "And Georgi will come home for lunch. Don't worry."

"We'll stay until your brother gets here, and then go on."

"And where will Miklos take you after that?"

"Back to her hotel to pick up her things," he supplied.

"And then?" I demanded.

"To Crete. You're coming home with me," he said. "My parents will take you in for tonight, until your reservation at your hotel there opens up."

He stared at me, looking so determined and so appealing that I couldn't resist him. The small hope that perhaps we'd lose the creep that was following me insisted on directing my steps, like a will-of-the wisp that led to nowhere. I took in a deep breath.

"All right," I agreed after a few seconds. "We'll go to Crete."

Chapter Seven

When we got back to my hotel the lobby attendant gave me some mail after I had finished checking out. I thanked him, wondering what it could be. But when I looked at the postmark I saw that my mother had sent it days ago, even before she got married. She wanted it to reach me here before I left Athens, apparently. There was a flat box with an envelope on top. I opened the envelope without much curiosity; it was probably last words of instruction and advice. But as was becoming common to me in recent times, I was in for a surprise. The letter was long for my mother and I nodded at Miklos, indicating that I wanted to sit down to read it.

"Read your letter," he said, leading me over to a little sofa that was settled under a sunny window in the lobby. I allowed the peace to settle as I unfolded it.

Dear Therese,

I guess this is the time for changes, and in packing up our house, I feel strange. Somehow I know that I won't be coming back here, at least not for a long time, if ever. This is your house now, as should go to my daughter. You haven't heard me call you that very often, but that's another change I've been going through. There's something to be said for growing older, and settling down at last. You may not believe it, but I'm very happy. Xavier is what I've always wanted, not only a man that I'm attracted to and who finds me beautiful, but he's a man I can turn to, laugh with, and even ignore! And so I've included your name on the deed to this house we've both called home. No matter what I'm doing, I want you to have a place to fall back on. There isn't much money to go with it, I'm afraid. I was never one for working, or expending too much time on investments.

So boring! And yet I'm proud of how I made my inheritance stretch until now. I got you through college, didn't I? And you have a degree, after all. I can't imagine why you took it in Education, but if that's what makes your flowers bloom I say go after it.

Meanwhile, even though I'm such a free spirit, never say that I can't be practical. Xavier makes a comfortable living, and I think I'm going to enjoy being a housewife, and entertaining neighbors and inviting the ladies over for coffee. I've perfected the hairstyle, a smooth chignon. And during the summer months, I intend to make my husband take me to tropical vacations, so I can dazzle him with how I look in a bikini, and remind him of how lucky he is to have married me.

Now I'll arrive at the reason I'm writing you this letter. I hope you won't feel I'm a coward for not telling you in person. But since I'm so willing to change, I might as well unlock a few secrets.

It always amazed me, Therese that you were never curious as to who your father was. I didn't mean to keep him from you, really. I had thought I would let him see you, as often as he wanted to. And he never asked. He's that sort of man, you see. He was done with me, and he doesn't like to feel entangled in an ended relationship. He didn't know I was pregnant when we broke up, and he never saw you. And so it made it easy for him to dispel his responsibility to you by sending you money. All those years he never once sent you a personal message or acknowledged the school photos of you that I sent. Four years ago, when you turned eighteen, the money stopped coming. That was the last I heard of him, and I shrugged and let it go. I'd never spent any of the money he sent, anyway. I put it away, and forgot about it.

But here's the odd thing, a week ago, not long after you told me you were going to Greece, I got a letter from the man after all these years. And perhaps you get your desire for education from him. It seems he's become some sort of famous scientist, in the field of bio-chemical experimentation, or something like that. He said he wanted to meet you. He sent some money, enough for any arrangements that need to be made. His handwriting looked different, but perhaps he's changed as much as I have. When I saw where he was located I thought it even stranger. Sweet pea, he's there in Greece, on some small island or other. Life all comes around and makes sense in the end, even to someone as flighty as me. So go on and look him up, if you want to. Wire him first, to let him know when to expect you. I've given you his address on the back of this page.

Also remember to write to me and tell me all about it. Your father, if I may say so, was quite a looker, and it's from him that you got your coloring. He had that thick, dark red hair, and those dusty herbal eyes. It sounds better when I'm describing a man! But you got my figure, too, didn't you, Pet? You may as well show it off to that man of yours that you write to. I've sent you a present, and I'll have you know that I shopped for it and thought of you while you were lying around sick nibbling on snacks and reading magazines. That's my girl!

Love, June

A range of emotions shook me as I broke open the little cardboard box, and reaching in I pulled out some soft material. I held it up, revealed in the sunshine. It was a trendy bikini, with gold and bright white stripes, and little ties at the cotton hips. I couldn't help myself, I laughed while I shook my head. What a legacy!

Of course Miklos took that moment to appear, walking forward with his eyes staring at the two spare pieces of fabric. I saw him and yanked them down, clutching them into my lap.

"Very nice," he commented.

"A gift from my mother."

His eyebrows elevated, but I took that moment to scramble to my feet with my mother's letter.

"Miklos, my mother wrote me ... I don't know what to think."

I put a confused hand to my forehead.

"Now what's wrong?"

"Here," I said, sitting back down, "read it."

He lowered to the couch beside me. It took a few moments for him to digest it, and I sat and studied the changes of expression on his face. I loved watching the corners of his mouth move, and the long spiky eyelashes. His eyes lifted and caught me staring.

"I remember your mother from when we were children," he said, with a smile. "She seems just the same."

I shook my head.

"This letter is very different, for her. Imagine how long she had to sit still, just to write it. That's not like my mother at all."

"And what will you do? You must visit your father, of course?"

I frowned.

"I don't see why I should; after all, he never wanted to visit me. He didn't even ask me to visit with his own letter addressed to me. He went through my mother instead, and he must have known the risks involved there. I don't think I want to meet him."

"But, Therese, he's family."

I looked up, seeing that he sounded agitated. I bit my lip, glad that family was important to him, and yet never more aware that I didn't know what life in a family unit was like. I had no grandparents, or siblings or aunts or uncles. Just a mother who, invariably, wanted to play girlish games for longer than I did. I lowered my head.

"I don't know how to wish for a father," I said into my lap. He chuckled and I raised my gaze.

"But he's wishing to see you," he pointed out. "And of course he must want to see you face to face. Especially if he got the same school photos of you that I did."

"Oh, yes, so appealing. Brown-red hair and a funny smile!"

"But I don't know any other redheads."

I took a deep breath.

"Well, since you're such a good friend, I'll let you influence me. Where's my father staying? Do you recognize the address?"

He turned the letter over and studied the address with a frown.

"Hmm," he said. "I'm sorry to say I don't recognize this island, Therese, and I run boats for a living."

"Maybe it's a small town way up the mountains in the north, and that's why you don't recognize it."

"No, you see this word in parenthesis, nisi, that means island."

"But don't you know all the islands?"

"There are many islands in Greece. Some are very small. It's said that when God was finished creating the Earth that he ..."

"Threw out the leftover rocks and that was Greece, yes, I've heard that one."

"Well, it sounds better than that."

"I didn't memorize the adage. I read it on the plane."

"How would you like it if I asked, 'Say, does the Star Spangled Banner wiggle over there?'"

His voice droned in an imitation southern Texas accent.

"Pardon me," I grinned. "I'll try to do better."

He stood up, my letter clutched in his hand as he bent to pick up my cases.

"We'll figure it out, Pouli. We'll go see my family first, and that will make you wish to see your father."

I thought back to twelve years ago.

"I remember your parents, Miklos. They were very nice to me."

"Then come on. My friend says I can leave this car in Piraeus and he'll pick it up there. We'll take the ferry. It's a nine hour trip, though, to get to Crete."

"Lead on. I'm ready for a new adventure."

Chapter Eight

"Ka lee neck ta," I said. "Good night."

"Kali NEEK ta," he corrected. I grinned.

"Kali neck tie!"

"Now you're being silly."

"I'm not. No. Oh chi."

"OH shee."

"Ah. And how do you say 'thank you' again?"

"Efkharisto."

"Ef ca wrist TOE!"

"Ef kah rees TO."

I mumbled to myself for a minute, trying to remember.

"I don't know why this is so hard," he put in. "You knew all these words when we were children."

"Because of a basic flaw in your letter writing; you never reminded me."

"I was too busy dealing with floods of English."

"I had a lot to tell you."

He smiled and looked out over the water, and I enjoyed the way the wind played in his hair. We were on the ferry, sitting back from the rail but out on deck. We had talked for hours, and it was getting late. Tomorrow I would be in Crete, at the home of his parents and then a few days later at the hotel that Xavier had arranged for me. My plan to stay in Greece for two months was just beginning. And yet I felt a disquiet that I didn't want to share with Miklos. My thoughts drifted to that stubby-haired mute who had violated my privacy at my hotel and then had shaken me outside of Accalia's apartment. The man had been so calm, and so deliberate. He had chosen to enter my room and wake me, and had chosen to shake me, too. Was he just toying with me? Was he the sort who enjoyed frightening a woman when he had a free afternoon? But no. He had entered my examination room in Seattle. He had flown over here on my plane. Put a check mark also on him locating my hotel room and where I went to stay that night. This man was following me, and I'd be silly if I didn't acknowledge it. From Seattle to here, he had a purpose in keeping tabs on me. Suddenly I shivered. He might be with us somewhere, right now on this ferry.

"Are you cold?" my friend asked.

"A little, but I don't want to go inside. I like it out here in the wind."

He was amenable, and a moment later I was very content, discharging any unsettling thoughts about bulky-shouldered strangers. Miklos had opened his sports coat and wrapped me close to his side for warmth. We sat together, quiet now, and watched the waves toss and curl in front of the ferry.

It seemed like Miklos' entire family was there to meet us at Heraklion when we pulled into port. I was very happy to recognize his parents. It had only been twelve years, after all, and they looked much the same. A little softer around the edges, but still the same welcoming arms, which were open to me now.

"Oh, look at our little American friend." his mother said.

"She hasn't grown up yet." from his father. "She is too thin."

"I'm surprised you remember me, Mr. Iasonas," I grinned. "You only knew me for three weeks."

"Of course we remember you. We've read all your letters."

I sent a glance over at Miklos, but he was conveniently busy greeting his three-year-old nephew.

"Come and ride in our car," his mother continued, and on the way there we established that I should call her Brizo.

"Breez-zo,"

"Very good," she congratulated.

Two cars took off from the Ferry dock, both full of happy, chattering Greeks, and me.

That car ride settled something inside me. I felt as if I were seeing these people on several levels, making assumptions based on my own experiences from my childhood vacation, and also on what I expected the loving Greek family to act like in front of a visitor from America. I wondered if it was real, if they were always this courteous of each other, and always this awake. For somehow all my energy was draining away. I felt like I had no words, and no spark. My illness, tucked away till now, reemerged, reminding me that I was tired, that drawing breath was more taxing. I held in a yawn and felt a powerful urge to lean my head back and sleep. Mr. Iasonas was driving; I was next to him in the middle of the front seat while Brizo was at the window. In the back seat was Miklos' brother Myron, his wife, whose name I had forgotten, their two children on laps, and Taisa, Miklos' cousin.

They were talking around me now, about politics, and the new ferry system of ANEK. Most of the time they spoke in English, but after a while they relaxed and focused on their own language. I smiled at everyone, nodding and trying to show my appreciation, while my eyes drooped. I yawned again, and then apologized. I was forgiven before the words were out of my mouth.

What was wrong with me? I should have been excited, for at last I had reached a destination that secretly I had desired for years. And then the answer came.

I felt safe. That's why I wanted to sleep. In all the bustle and uncertainty of the last few days, in the middle of these people I knew I could let go of the anxiety that had been bothering me more than I'd realized.

Then his mother felt that I wasn't being represented enough in conversation and began asking me questions about my trip. That helped. By the time we reached the neighborhood by the beaches on the outskirts of Heraklion I was feeling better.

"There it is!" I exclaimed, as soon as the car turned a corner, and the vacation home that I remembered so well appeared in front of me. My mother had rented a little house that summer, and it was still standing, still painted the same color even.

"I remember there was a funny closet in my bedroom at that house," I told them. "I could climb up through a hole at the top of the shelf. I crawled through some rafters, and there I found a circle window, and from it I could reach the roof."

Myron spoke from the back seat.

"You could not have reached the roof from that small circle window," he said. "The roof of that house extends out right above it."

"Yes, but there's a beam that sticks out under the window," I turned in the seat, excited to explain to him. "It looks like a perch for some giant bird. I stood up on that, and then I could climb onto the roof."

"It's amazing that Miklos was called upon to save your life only once," Myron replied. "Did you spend all your time on our island taking such risks?"

I laughed, while his mother scolded him for sounding impolite. But I liked it. I remembered that Myron was three years older than Miklos, and so I hadn't spent much time with him that vacation.

"I'm sorry, Therese," the man apologized with an eye on his mother. Beside him, his wife spoke in Greek, and he replied. I turned and looked at her. She was a small person, who seemed as young as I. She had bright eyes, and a smile that looked as if she had a continual pleasant secret that she was keeping to herself. Her dark brown hair was short, cut close to her head like a boy's, except for the occasional, and adorably distracting, curl. She had on a dress like what I used to wear in grade school, simple cotton, with a button blouse collar. My smile grew for her.

"Please forgive me," I said to her, "but I've forgotten your name." Her pleasant secret lit her eyes to include me.

"My name is Alceste," she told me.

"All sest."

"Yes."

"And look there, Therese," Miklos' father interrupted. "There's our home. We've swept out Miklos' old room for you to stay in."

"Where will Miklos sleep?"

"He doesn't live here anymore. He lives in Heraklion, closer to his business."

I nodded, feeling even better. That man who stole Miklos' letters didn't have this address as the current one. I'd found a hideaway here, like when I was a child and had crawled through a hole to climb out on the roof and see the stars.

Mr. Iasonas came to a stop, and we all climbed out. The house in front of me was cheerful, with whitewashed walls and a blue door. There was a tarp lean-to off the side, bringing some shade to that part of the house. Behind us was the sand mixed with rock that made up the beach, and as a backdrop, the water.

"So beautiful," I murmured.

The other car pulled up, and out from it came Miklos' little sister, a girl of eleven I hadn't met when I came as a child, three of his cousins, his aunt, her husband, and Miklos himself. The uncle walked up to me and spoke, but his English was merely Greek directed at me. He pulled out a cigarette and lit it, blowing smoke. As I stood and greeted the others again, the smoke crawled toward me on an errant draft, and went the wrong way into my lungs.

A coughing fit came to humiliate me. I backed away, embarrassed.

And then Miklos was beside me, his hand warm on my shoulder as he looked back and told his family that he would take me on a little walk to see the water. I held in the cough and excused myself. My eyes were watering and my breath short as he pulled me along.

"Come over here, Pouli," he said. "The air is fresh."

"Miklos, this cough is stupid," I complained, bringing it under control.

"Coughs are not smart or dumb."

"This one is. It comes right when I want to appear normal."

"You are normal."

I rubbed one eye with the back of my fingers.

"Are you all right? You look pale."

I shook my head and focused out. The light, it was high, and the air ruffled and flowed like small waves. Discomfort lifted, like a burden taken away.

"I'm happy to be here, Miklos. This beach, I don't know if this makes any sense, but it feels as if a part of me never left here."

"A part of you did remain here. You almost lost your life out in those waters."

"Like the legend about a cat having nine lives? You think I left a life behind here?"

"Your life changed that day. In nearly ending, a beginning was made."

"Trying to be a poet?"

"Perhaps I'm trying to impress you."

"No need. I was plenty impressed when I was ten and you pulled me out of the water and kissed me."

"I wasn't kissing you. You weren't breathing."

"Allow a girl to see things from her own perspective."

"Are you flirting with me, little Pouli?"

"Not yet, Romeo."

He grinned.

Chapter Nine

It was Alceste who took me to my room, or, what used to be Miklos' room. In a back corner of the house, it was a small square room, with bright sunshine as decoration. A bed, a closet enclosure, a lamp that had tiles at its base, and a few other things that spoke of its former occupant. I liked it right away. High between the edge of the window and the wall, a small shelf had been made, and here were some books. I took one down, its hard cover was warm and the book was heavy with thick shiny paper.

But it was in Greek, and although I looked at the black and white photos inside that went along with the written pages with great curiosity, I would need Miklos to explain why the book was here.

"Do you think you will be comfortable?"

I turned and smiled at Alceste.

"Very comfortable."

"Miklos said you would be tired and I should encourage you to rest for a few hours."

"We were up all night on the ferry."

"And yet, there's something more wrong with you, no?"

I felt pensive, and she must have seen it on my face.

"I've been around someone sick, you see," she said simply.

"I have been sick, but I'm getting better now."

"You've seen the doctors?"

"I have. They prescribed some place dry and warm. Seattle, where I live, has a lot of rain all year long."

"And so you came to see Miklos."

That smile of hers would lead a bird to a gilded cage.

"Yes," I went along. "I came to visit Miklos. It was time."

She nodded and sat down at a little chair in the corner.

"Tell me about your bedroom in Seattle. It has more in it than this one, I think."

I put my bag down and sat on the bed, relieving my hair of its tie and getting comfortable.

"My house is about the same size as this one," I told her. "But only two bedrooms."

"So you don't have a large family?"

"Just my mother and I. At least... well, she just got married. I guess I'll be on my own when I get back."

She shook her head.

"Living alone, I can't imagine it. I stayed at home until I got married, four years ago."

"Forgive me, but you seem young to have two children."

"I'm twenty-three, but yes, I was young. I had to have Myron, and I saw no sense in waiting."

I liked the way she pronounced her husband's name, although I would have said it the same way, it sounded more graceful with her accent.

"You know English very well," I commented.

"I'm good with languages. I speak French also."

"I'm impressed. Je parle Francais, mais jus'que' un peu."

She laughed at my broad American attempt.

"Are you sure that was correct?" she said.

"Well, maybe not," I agreed, and we both laughed together.

"You're nice," she said, with a tilt of her head.

"Nice enough to get to know Miklos?"

That secret smile slanted her mouth again.

"You're smart too," she added, and then nodded as she got up. "You'll need to be, if you want to interest Miklos."

"Who said I want to interest him?"

"He's Myron's little brother, no?"

Who could argue with such logic? She went to the door.

"Thank you, Alceste," I said, "for taking the time to speak to me. I hope we can spend some more time together. We could go shopping, perhaps."

Her eyes lit.

"I'd like that," she said. "I can show you all the best places to buy your souvenirs. You can get your mother something. Would she like a new apron?"

I managed to hold in my laugh. I knew what I intended to buy my mother, but I wasn't sure that Alceste would understand; a cute, Grecian, and modest bikini.

"Uh ... something like that," I said.

After Alceste went out I tried to rest as Miklos advised. I looked at my watch. It was only noon, and I felt strange. Jet lag was catching up to me I supposed, two days after arrival. I went and stood at the window, and looked at his back yard. It was different than mine had been back home. Seattle was vibrant with green color, and distances there were filled with points of interest, buildings and hills and streets and if you were situated in the city correctly, a water or mountain view.

His back yard in Greece was different. The landscape here was a variety of tans, beiges, off-whites and blues. Back home peace could be found in a mild climate, the sun had no glare, and the rain was often a gentle mist. But here there was peace in the steadiness of antiquity, the warmth of the light and the air, and the firm rock beneath my feet.

I stood there until my shoulders began to ache from weariness. When I lay down, the cough came almost immediately. I sat up, waiting for the fit to pass. I was tense, frustrated, and uncertain. I was a guest here, but I didn't know this family's rhythms. What were the ladies of the household doing? Where was Miklos? Was he working with his father or brother? Was Alceste in the kitchen laughing and chatting with the other ladies? They were all busy and I didn't know what to do. My eyes narrowed as I noticed that his window could open, and it would be an easy climb for my feet to touch the smooth rock pavement outside.

I carried my sandals in my hand and ventured down and away from their house. And soon I was a few hundred yards away; at the beach house my mother had rented for our vacation twelve years ago. There was no car in the drive and no activity at any of the windows. But I resisted the temptation to peer in the glass. Instead I went down to the water, feeling the wind now that it was picking up. There was a rock wall nearby and I settled against it, letting it guard me from the chill.

It was there that I thought about my father. My mother was right. When I'd been a child I never asked about him. But I had listened. I'd attended to my mother's idle comments. I'd gathered impressions from her of him, of a distracted man, and a busy one, who had taken a moment to pause his pace for a fling with my mother. She'd shown him that he had hidden passions that he'd embraced with curiosity. But neither one of them had been ready for a serious relationship. She'd said that outright, more than once. My mother was astute at times. They had wanting, and hunger for each other. But there'd been no driving dream of a future together to back it up.

This disjointed message about my father had never satisfied me. Was that all he was? Could his value be summed up this way? What if there was far more to him? Perhaps he was still a looker, and had accepted his passions. Maybe he laughed with his friends and cried when he was sad. Maybe there was a part of him, however small, that regretted never knowing me.

The thought brought a few agitated tears that surprised me. And then they annoyed me. What was going on anyway? This was my trip, a dream fulfilled. But that message from my mother telling me that my father wanted to see me had troubled me. I wiped my tears and sat up straight. With silence I stared out over the water, and incidentally at the distant spot where I went under and Miklos had jumped in to save me those years ago.

I heard no other sounds close by, at least not human sounds. There was only the thrum of the wind, the stroke of the water's waves. My skirt ruffled against my legs, and my hair lifted from my face. The dusty rock-sand underneath me felt as if I could own a bit of this place. The world was not spinning and I wasn't lost. As I felt more grounded I began to relax. I set my arms back against the wall and rested my cheek on them. I could breathe propped up like this. My eyes drifted closed.

I startled awake because someone had shouted my name right next to me. I opened my eyes to see Miklos standing over me.

"Therese, there you are!" he exclaimed, sounding irritated. I rubbed my face and got oriented. I blinked in shock. The sun was low in the sky, preparing for a wondrous sunset before it went down in a few hours. I glanced at my watch and scrambled to my knees. It was after four o'clock. I had slept for hours.

"Argh!" Miklos said, grabbing the back of his head. "Do you know what you've done to me!"

"No, what?" I asked, upset that he seemed upset.

"I went into your room, a half an hour ago to see if you needed anything before dinner. You weren't there!"

I got up.

"I apologize," I hurried to say. I could picture what had happened.

"Therese, I've been running up and down this beach asking shopkeepers ... I couldn't see you behind this wall! Were you trying to hide from me?"

"No, I'm sorry. I didn't mean to fall asleep."

He swiped his fingers down his nose and over his chin.

"I wondered if you had gone out in the water," he went on, his voice low. "I wondered if you'd never learned to swim any better than you did when you were that skinny little girl that used to follow me around."

I got a little fed up.

"Well, I'm not stupid whatever else I am."

"But you weren't there."

"I'm here now."

"I also wondered if some strange man had come for you," he added.

The words made me swallow. I studied him as he stood in front of me. He had on shorts now, and his brown legs were sturdy. He was wearing a polo shirt that accented his strong but slender torso. The top button was undone and I saw the skin under his throat. He had a beard starting, and his tousled hair was shaggy with the wind coming from behind. And those eyes of his, with the darker lashes. My gaze lowered to the lean brown hands. Something inside me grew hungry, and my arms crossed over my chest.

I wasn't ready for more at the moment, and I turned away, to look out over the water.

"Therese?"

"Yes, I'm sorry," I repeated to the waves. "I didn't mean to worry you."

"No, I'm sorry. I shouldn't have yelled at you. My mother would be shocked if she saw me treat a guest this way."

That got a reaction.

"Oh, no, please don't. Don't make me a guest again. Let's just be friends, Miklos. Nothing more and no pressure. I want you to yell at me."

He stared and then chuckled.

"Are all American girls this strange," he teased, walking up and directing my shoulders back toward his house, "or is it just you, Pouli?"

Chapter Ten

Hours after the noisy, vibrant, and abundant meal began with the Iasonas family, we left the table. Those of us who hadn't imbibed too much or who weren't so young that they had to go to bed discussed the future of my next few days. The family had become investigators during dinner, asking me all about my mother's recent wedding, my days at College, if I had any boyfriends, and all about the rest of my family. It seemed to be hard for them to accept that I had very little family to speak of. My mother had a few cousins, and that was all. It was natural that they turned to exploring the possibility of me meeting my father since he was right here in Greece.

"Let's see your mother's letter again," Myron said, and I, having long since gotten over feeling as if I had any secrets from my new friends, complied without hesitation.

"I think this is in the Aegean Islands," Myron said, studying the address.

Miklos reached over from where he sat beside me on a couch and took the paper from him.

"Ah yes," he said a moment later. "I recognize this now. The address lists an island nearby to Skyros."

"Skyros?" I asked. "Where's that?"

"Its north, Pouli. One of the larger islands in the Sporades group." He grinned. "Too far to drive, like you do in America."

"Ah, but you're a man with a boat," I pointed out, but he held up his hands and laughed.

"My friend and I own a small yacht, you might call it, a boat for passengers to be comfortable with a motor. And we own a few fishing boats designed to impress tourists. We don't own a luxury liner. Unless you want a journey of hundreds of miles."

"How would I get there, then?"

"You could fly into Thessaloniki," Mr. Iasonas said. "You would be much closer then, and could find your way to this small island from there. Or perhaps you could travel to Euboea from Athens."

I leaned my head back, feeling too comfortable after three glasses of wine to contemplate traveling anywhere very far.

"Or perhaps I could wire my father and make him come to me," I said, my voice sounding a little sloppy. My eyes began to feel heavy. I giggled. "Can you imagine it? Him running my way with his brown-red hair and his herbal green eyes?"

"Hmmm," Miklos said. "I think perhaps this young woman has had enough wine."

"No," I told him. "Oh shheee. I haven't had enough. I mean I haven't had too much."

"I'll help her," put in Alceste.

"No, I will," insisted Miklos' mother. In the end Taisa volunteered too, and I wished the gentlemen, who were a little floaty to look at, an American goodnight.

"Oh, she has a pretty nightgown!" said Taisa a few minutes later. She was holding up my peach-colored chiffon baby-doll pajamas with the puff sleeves.

"We mustn't let Miklos see her in that so soon," Alceste replied, her smile of secrets up to full power. "He has to earn it first."

Brizo scolded her daughter-in-law but laughed as she said something in Greek.

"I'm fully capable of dressing myself," I stated in a formal tone, but I held the peach jammies up to Taisa and nodded. "I'll give this to you, if you like it," I told her, but none of them took me seriously. Soon I was helped to undress, and my second nightgown, which was white with a small V-neck, was on me. Brizo sat me down and began to pull a brush through my hair.

I took a deep relaxing breath, watching the other two ladies drift around my room, folding my recently worn clothes, setting my make-up bag by the table, even taking out my lotion and smoothing it into my hands and my face. I was tipsy, but I knew that I was making a memory at this moment, and one that I wouldn't forget. Brizo put the brush down and went and folded down the bed, and the three of them went to the door.

"Goodnight, Therese," they said, and I thanked them. Climbing into bed I knew I could sleep tonight, and not just because of the wine. My chest and my lungs were relaxed as well. I snuggled down, turning off the lamp with the little tiles at the base and watching the window as it glowed with light blue moonlight. My eyes grew too heavy to keep open and I slept.

I woke up early, and felt a little groggy. I was thankful that I wasn't hung over. I got cleaned up and put on a new sundress I had bought in Seattle, dreaming of hot weather. I considered wearing the new bikini my mother had gotten for me underneath, but I put it down with a laugh and put on a more modest offering instead. I slipped on my sandals and ignoring whatever Miklos might think, climbed out the bedroom window.

In the backyard I encountered his father, who was busying himself by tinkering with a motor. We shared a few pleasant words and I went on, broadening my step as the beach beckoned, and arriving at the water's edge after a brisk walk. I shaded my eyes with my hand against the morning sun. Heraklion, about ten miles from this village, could be seen from here. I looked the other direction and soaked in the lush green of the plant life and the piercing blue of the sky. Some children were focused on the sand not far away, and I realized that here were tourists. My eyes followed the line behind the children up to the guesthouse that my mother had rented those years ago. These children were probably from there.

I smiled to myself. Was there a young Miklos somewhere around? Was there a local boy to this village who for some inexplicable reason was willing to befriend a lonely child building sandcastles all by herself? I bit my lip. I didn't like the feeling. Why did I think I was special? Wasn't I just temporary to Miklos' life, a cross-section bigger than other tourists got, it was true, but still just one child in a long list of tourist children?

I slipped off my sandals and entered the water, just until the hem of my dress was threatened with moisture. I thought of my mother, someplace else on the earth, on some other beach. She had, with all of her Peter Pan tendencies, the ability that those children behind me had. She could play, and laugh and own every beach she came to. She didn't worry about whether she belonged or what the locals thought of her. She didn't wonder if perhaps she was being tolerated, with a pat on the head for being appealing. I gathered up my skirts and ventured further in, until I was wet above the knees. Almost I pulled the dress off and swam, for I was wearing my swimsuit. But it was cold, for the early morning sun hadn't brought its heat yet. If I were my mother I would go back and luxuriate over breakfast. I would do my hair and my make-up, and then I would select the best bikini for the job, no matter if any promising men showed up or not.

But I wasn't her. I ambled, back to the shore, and over to the wall where I had napped yesterday. I sat on it and swung my legs, waiting for my feet to dry. No one came to find me on the deserted early morning beach. No Miklos, either a look-alike of twelve, or the grown man himself, walked up and asked what I was doing.

All of a sudden it hit me. I was a young, independent woman, who owned a home, had several thousand dollars in the bank given to me by an errant father, and a degree which would guarantee me prospects of a job when I decided I needed it. I was reasonably attractive, well-read and free. No one could stop me or tell me what to do. And if Miklos cared to try, he'd find out that he was dealing with a girl who was well able to take care of herself.

I felt better. I got up, and turned to go back to the Iasonas family with an offer to help with breakfast. But I looked up and froze instead, dismay jarring over my nerves.

A man stood on the beach, fifteen feet away. He was wearing casual clothes, cotton pants and a short-sleeved shirt. His arms were ridiculous widths of muscle, and not the pretty kind that turned a woman's head. His stubby blond hair stood out against the pink-red of his fair skin. I felt a wild urge to run up and kick him as hard as I could in the shin. But I yelled at him instead, repeating the same questions I always asked of him.

"What are you doing here? What do you want?"

My shriek in the peaceful silence of playing children and searching birds slashed the air. I turned and hurried away from him. But he was fast, and he grabbed me from behind right when we were level with the children. Sand was kicked in their direction and I was appalled. I tried to wrench away from him, but he grasped onto my arms with clamp fingers.

The children, shocked at first, backed away when I began to fight with frenzy. They disappeared into the distance, their voices calling for their mother in French. The fellow began dragging me now, up the sand, toward the road. I kicked my assailant in the shins like I had wanted to before.

I looked over in desperation. This was his cue. Miklos was supposed to see, somehow to know and be concerned. But I knew I didn't want the Miklos that I pretended him to be. I wanted to get to know the real man, and then to decide if we would be friends. I didn't exist because of him, and I also wasn't to be dragged off by this other fellow like my own life meant nothing.

I plowed my feet in the sand, leaving big grooves. I screamed, loud and piercing, and then breathless and with little power. As the road neared I used my head and sank, becoming a heavy weight the man picked up to heft. That gave me kicking room as he swung me high to clear the sand. His arms were folded around my waist and I kicked with viciousness. At last I earned the first sound the brute had ever made to me. He grunted, and then, with a roar once my flying heel connected below the belt, he got mad. He threw me down so he could deal with me.

But I was a live wire, and his grasping hands couldn't clench onto anything but the material of my skirt. He tore it right from the seam as I ripped away. But I had to let it go and be free. My humiliation burned as adrenalin made me run faster. My skirt was gone and I was wearing nothing much but the top of my sundress and the bottoms of my red and well-worn two-piece swimsuit. My face was open in distress. I was scratched from his paw-like hands. And I had to go back to the house of my friends and bring this trouble and my shame upon them.

I threw a glance behind me and saw the evil man's car pulling away from the guesthouse where he had parked. He must've decided to cut his losses before I got help. But I ran to the side of the house, the one without the lean-to that had a few tools and hid against the wall. I couldn't bear to have Miklos's father see me with the violence written all over my face. I clamped my hand over my mouth and sank down to the ground. On this unpopulated side of the house, my only hope was that no one would find me.

Chapter Eleven

After a while I removed my torn dress, steadied my expression, and walked to the back of the house in my swimsuit, carrying the rest. I sent Mr. Iasonas a casual wave as I climbed in the window. He barely noticed me and went back to his puttering.

But I leaned against the bedroom wall and shook all over. In reality less than fifteen minutes had passed since I was attacked. The blond man had driven away, removing himself from the area and any possible pursuit.

Many thoughts passed through my head, but the one that surfaced surprised me. For the first time in my life, I wanted a father. I wanted someone to go to, lay down my problems and allow him to figure out the solution. All through my childhood my mother had avoided dealing with problems. She paid the bills so debtors wouldn't come. She kept the noise down so neighbors wouldn't complain. And she gave in to me whenever possible so I wouldn't pressure her. I yearned for someone to turn to now, a parent who provided a haven. But I had to be stronger than that. I reached in my bag and pulled out my mother's letter with shaking fingers. The island of Skyros ...

At breakfast I announced my intention. I was going to Skyros to find my father. A lot of advice flew around, but I noticed that Miklos remained silent and let his family ask the questions. Afterward he asked me if I'd like to take a walk with him. I thought of the beach and repressed a shiver.

"I'd rather go on a drive," I said. "I don't remember much of the scenery around here."

Soon we were outside, but we weren't to go driving in the car. Mr. Iasonas was still working on it. Instead Miklos pulled a plain white motorcycle out of a shed. I climbed up behind him with eagerness, glad that the sun had become warm. We waved at his brother and Alceste as he bumped us out of the driveway onto the winding little street. I clamped onto his waist and the wind ruffled my hair loose from the sides of its ponytail, but Miklos didn't go too fast. I kept glancing behind us, but I saw no one and relaxed.

We drove south through a few other villages, but at last he found a nice spot of beach in between and we clambered down a steep hill to get to the water. Miklos held my hand until I had climbed over some angled rocks, and then I sat on the edge of one and smiled up at him.

"You seem different this morning, Pouli," he observed.

I nodded.

"I've made a decision."

"To visit your father."

"Yes. Don't you think it's a good idea?"

He shrugged.

"Is your life," he said, perching himself to sit next to me on the rocks.

"But?"

He looked out over the water, and then threw a pebble into the distance. I heard the pebble's tiny splash.

"But you came here to rest, didn't you? I heard you coughing in the night."

"I was? Strange, but I was sleeping so deep I never woke all the way up to realize I was coughing, I guess." I smiled over at him. "The result of all that wine."

We fell into a short silence.

"There's something different about you this morning," he stated suddenly. "I want to know what's wrong."

"Wrong? What seems wrong?"

"You're like those letters you were writing me before your mother got married. There was no spark in those letters. No life."

"Well, I'm certainly alive," I said in a dry tone.

"Tell me, Pouli." His voice was firm, and the request was simple. I bit my lip.

The silence stretched between us again and I felt the restless jerk of his arm as another pebble was shot into space.

"I ... don't want to involve you," I admitted at last.

"Involve me in what?"

"I don't know."

"Therese."

"Well, I don't."

"This has something to do with that man, doesn't it? The one who shook you outside my friend Georgi's apartment?"

He sure was smart, I thought, admiring him.

"Yes, it does. He's following me, Miklos."

"You don't know that."

"It can't be a coincidence. I saw him four times before we came here, and he took your letters."

"Tell me the rest. Something changed this morning inside you. Why?"

I bit my lip again, blinking at the intensity in his eyes.

"Well ..."

He waited, like some handsome Greek statue. Even his hair wasn't ruffled by the wind. I expelled my breath and spilled it.

"I saw that man on the beach this morning," I admitted. Miklos reared up, onto his knees in the sand to face me on my level.

"You saw him here!"

"Yes. I climbed out your window and was watching some children build sandcastles. I turned around and there he was."

"Did he say anything to you?"

I swallowed, but Miklos reached out and took my shoulders in a gentle but demanding grip.

"Therese!"

"He's bad, Miklos. He scared those little children. He ripped my dress."

Torrents of Greek sentences spoken eloquent and fast made my eyes widen.

"You're swearing at me again," I whispered.

"He grabbed you?"

"Yes. From behind."

"And then?"

"I kicked him in his private parts."

I said this with relish.

"And then?"

"He grunted and threw me down, and I ran away."

"Are you all right?"

"A few scratches and a bruise or two. He was trying to drag me over to his car, I think. Whatever this man is after, he's escalating his efforts. I don't want your family to be next on the menu."

The phrase distracted him.

"'Next on the menu?'"

"Like a meal has courses, you know."

"Greek meals don't have courses."

"First an appetizer, then a salad, then up to the main course ..."

He was nodding, and growing thoughtful.

"Yes, I understand. The main course is what?" he asked. "Are you sure you can't think of anything this person could want?"

"I've wracked my brains."

"'Wracked your brains?'"

"Tried to think."

He had to grin.

"It sounds painful."

I laughed, and he sat back again, with one knee bent up.

"I didn't know if I should tell you, Miklos."

"Why not?"

"Back to the beginning of this conversation, because I don't want you to get involved."

"How can I not be involved? I'm going with you to Skyros."

"Oh, but you can't."

"I can do whatever I like, little Pouli."

"But your job, I mean your business. Won't it suffer?"

"I'm not due back for over a week. Andros can handle things."

"Thank you for the kind thought but I don't want you to be hurt! Some things are best done by myself!"

"I'm your friend, right Therese? How can I let you go alone?"

I put my head down on my knees.

"I'm scared for you, Miklos. Maybe I should go back home."

"Home to your empty house?"

"Why say it like that?"

"Because you're safer here with us. Let this be your home for now, Therese."

"I think I need to find my father. Somehow I think there's a connection."

"Why do you think that?"

"Because all these years he didn't want to see me. Why now? And did you read that part of my mother's letter that said that his handwriting looked different?"

"You mean you think he didn't write the letter telling your mother he wanted to see you?"

"I think I need to find out. At any rate, it can't hurt to try. After all, if he did write that letter, perhaps he does want to see me. Maybe he could be a help to me."

"All right. You make sense. We'll go tomorrow."

"Are you sure?"

"Of course. You need help finding your way around. There are many islands in Greece. I don't want you to get lost on one."

It was a great comfort to have his sturdy shoulder by my side as we sat and decided to go. In the hot sunshine with the aqua blue sky in front of us, it was hard to believe in any danger. After a while he pulled me over the rocks and we climbed back up to his motorcycle. Then we were off again, zooming along until we came to a village called Agioi Deka. Miklos told me it was named after ten men, who were martyred for being Christians back in 250 AD.

The village was beautiful; with so many old stone structures I was amazed. There was an old church built in 1250 AD, and we went inside. I marveled at huge pillars of glossy stone, ornate floors, ancient paintings depicted in the carved and impressive altar, and the beautiful wooden seats as pews. Outside we strolled to a tiny restaurant where we went in to have lunch.

The person who served us knew no English, and I smiled and nodded as Miklos gave the order and the man beamed back at me, talking in words I couldn't understand.

"He likes your red hair," Miklos told me once the man had gone.

After the meal we left and I looked carefully all around the little streets while Miklos backed up the motorcycle and started it for us. I climbed on and felt relief. I was certain that for this one afternoon the stubby-haired man had left us alone. We hadn't been followed.

I rested my head against his back shoulder blade as we returned to his village. I meshed myself against him, becoming one as he angled left and right around the curves. He rode around a corner and we were back, a few moments later the wheels bumped over the edge of the road and up to the shed where the motorcycle was stored.

"Thank you, Miklos," I said, holding out my hand. He took it, and l looked down at the brown veined skin of his hand. "I had a lovely time."

"I'm glad," he responded.

"Tomorrow we'll go back to Heraklion," I said.

"Yes. We'll go and make arrangements to travel."

I smiled and went inside ahead of him, hoping that it wasn't a mistake to bring him, and yet at the same time very happy that he was going. We'd find out what was going on. Or at least, we'd find my father.

Chapter Twelve

Just a few days after we'd left, we were flying back into Athens. The difference this time, there wasn't any plank-headed, tree-trunks for shoulders, blond man on the plane with me. I was determined to leave his shadow behind.

We went to a new hotel, called the Caravel, and had a dispute about the bill.

"Well of course I should pay for you," I insisted.

"I'm able to pay my own way."

"But you're here to help me."

"So am I your bodyguard, then, that you'll pay for me?"

"Ooo, yes! I like that idea. Can I order you to carry my cases and open doors for me?"

"I do that already."

"Then let me pay the bill."

"Perhaps I should pay for you instead."

"And what service do I render you? It sounds like you plan to do all the work."

"But that's the way of women, no?"

"Then why come if I'm so much trouble?"

He grinned.

"Because you're cute."

"I suppose you might be worth the money, Jeeves."

"Who is Jeeves?"

"Oh, never mind. I'm paying for this hotel. You carry up my cases."

"All right."

That settled we went to the large front desk in the modern looking hotel. It was fancy, but it was just overnight and we were assured of finding a room without a reservation. Tomorrow we would travel north, until we could catch a ferry to Skyros.

My room was several floors up, and my view, although it wasn't on the right side of the building to include the Acropolis, gave me the feeling of being perched in an eagle's nest. Athens was much larger of a city than I realized. It made me miss Seattle, but only for a moment.

We said we were going to dress for dinner, and I had told Miklos that a natural consequence to that decision was that I would need to go shopping. He came to my door and soon we had plunged into the streets of Athens. We took one of the gray-blue taxis, and the driver sized us up and delivered us to the perfect street of little shops. I chose a colorful orange and pink dress with a flowing skirt and a chiffon filmy layer over the top. I found some high-heeled platform sandals. Miklos bought himself a nice shirt. Back to the hotel we had time to shower before he came to my room and collected me to go down to the elegant restaurant attached to the hotel.

"For this dinner, I will pay," he had stressed.

It felt like a date. Was it? He said I was cute, didn't he? I dried my hair and brushed it until it shone. I sat down in front of the mirror in my room and applied my makeup. Using a finishing polish of gloss on my lips I stared at my reflection.

The color of the dress brought out the burnt umber in my hair. My eyes were delineated, and they appeared forest green with the eye shadow I had used. I brushed my hair up on my head and let a few strands grace the skin of my cheek. And last I pulled out my perfume, the one that I had made my own instead of borrowing it from my mother. I was bending down adjusting the strap on my sandal when he knocked and came in after I called entrance. I folded the tiny strap into the buckle at my ankle and looked up.

He was staring at me, and I liked the look in his eye. I came up to him and was just a few inches shorter than he in my heels. He pulled out a flower to give me, a small-budded, light pink rose.

"You look beautiful," he said.

The restaurant glowed with intimate candles at every table and tinkled with silver and china. The waiter spoke in hushed Greek-accented English. Miklos held my chair and I sat down, and took the tall menu with a gracious smile. I opened it and froze.

The Greek alphabet is similar looking in many ways. I always think that I could understand it, if I just studied it enough. I leaned forward and concentrated, until two lean brown fingers took hold of the other side. The menu lowered and I saw Miklos' grin.

"Wait Miklos. I think I want to order this." I showed him my choice, pointing my pink polished nail at the line of the menu that looked appealing. He looked down.

"You want squid marinated in Ouzo and olive sauce?"

"Here, you decide," I said, handing him the menu.

The waiter came back and Miklos reeled off the order. I smiled. It was easy to trust that he knew just what I wanted.

At the door of my room after dinner he stopped and smiled while I dug out my key.

"Thank you, Miklos, for dinner. But be careful. Being raised by my mother you never know what strange and expensive tastes I have underneath the surface."

"Much as I would like to say that I'm a rich man, I can't afford to take you out to a restaurant like that often," he replied.

"Lucky for you I'm not my mother," I told him. The door opened a few inches but I leaned against the wall. I wasn't sure if things should grow awkward.

"What are you thinking about, Pouli?"

"This evening felt like a date."

"And does that bother you?"

"It seems a little fast."

"And yet you dressed up for me, and bought those scary looking shoes."

"You're just not used to the idea of a woman being eye to eye with you."

He leaned a hand against the wall beside me.

"I'm still a little taller than you," he said.

"And I'm an independent girl of the seventies."

"So you are. Perhaps I like that about you."

"And what else about me do you like?"

"I like the fact that you're questioning this … thing between us."

"And you? Don't you have a few questions?"

"Yes. I'm wondering about something right now."

"And what's that?"

His gaze intensified, and his hand came up and stroked my

cheek.

"You want to slow down?" he asked.

With the warmth of his fingers on my skin I had serious doubts. It was several seconds before I overcame them.

"There's too much wrong with my life, Miklos. And not enough that's certain. I can't like you right till I know myself what I am."

"Now that," he said, dropping his fingers and standing straight, "is the vaguest answer a girl has ever given me."

"And has there been a lot of girls?"

"A few, but I'm not 'Romeo' as you called me."

"I called you Jeeves too."

"You're a Pouli, no matter how many fancy dinners you eat."

"And you're the best friend I have right now."

"You make it very hard," he complained.

"What do you mean?"

"Just go on in, and get some sleep. You're supposed to rest, and we keep forgetting that."

"Tomorrow we go on, Miklos. I can't rest now. I'll send my father a wire in the morning and see if he answers it before we catch the bus to Kymi at noon."

He sighed, but then stepped back so I could go inside my room.

"All right. I'll go with you. Good night, Therese."

"Good night, Miklos. And thank you."

He smiled with an uptilt to his lips. And then I surprised myself. Just as he turned to leave I grabbed him. Taking hold of his shirt I rose on my toes and tugged his head down. I kissed him, a searching contact that he took control of before I could pull away. One of his hands clamped behind my back and the other settled on my neck. My fingers ventured up into his tousled hair, something I had longed to do since the first moment I saw the loose curls at the Athens Airport when I arrived. He slowed the kiss, taking his time, changing the angles. I knew I should pull away, but it was just as I had thought it would be. My tastes were expensive indeed. I was craving the best, and he was giving it to me, and just because I asked.

That thought brought me back to ground. Those few girls he had mentioned. Had they done something similar to this? Had they grabbed on and hoped he would never lose interest in tasting their lips? I let out a sigh and he felt its softness on his mouth. His eyes opened, very close, and he took hold of my shoulders. I saw his throat move in a swallow, but for now he was staring at the wall above my head.

"I ... um ..." I stuttered.

"Shhh," he cut me off.

"I don't know where that came from except ..." I tried again.

"Except?"

"You didn't buy me any dessert," I complained at last.

"Dessert!"

"Well, maybe I was still hungry!"

He began to sound a little testy, and this time his hands took my upper arms. His kiss now was urgent, pressing and unforgettable. He pulled away like the snap of my mother's makeup case.

"Oh, no you don't, Pouli," he growled. "We're not having dessert until we reach the main course."

Now I was the one to swallow.

"The main course?" I repeated.

"You figure that out!"

"I'll try."

"And don't attack me again unless you want more than you're ready to deal with!"

"Yes, all right. I'm ..."

"Don't dare to apologize."

"No, okay, sorry."

I froze at the slip, but to my relief the look on my face must have amused him.

"Good night, Therese."

I slid to the door, anxious now to get in.

"Good night, Miklos!"

I said nothing more as I shut the door and leaned against the wall. As an afterthought I turned the lock. Whether to keep him out or myself in I wasn't sure.

Walking to the window I let the nighttime lights of Athens be the only thing that illuminated my room. It was late and I was recovering and I should get some sleep. But there was no way I could do that with the sensations pounding into me. It was a long time before my breath slowed back to its normal pace and I removed my clothes and slipped into my nightgown. I removed my makeup with my favorite cold cream, and brushed my hair. I put lotion on and then sat against the pillows of the bed, soaking myself in moonlight. It was the only lighting that seemed appropriate.

Chapter Thirteen

The bus ride to Kymi was awkward at first, but we relaxed after a while and began talking again. I decided that pretending the kiss never happened was a good idea. (Two kisses—my mind pointed out, but I silenced it.) Again there was no blond enemy to be found on my current transportation, and my spirits lifted even more. Perhaps the fellow was done following me. Maybe he decided I was too much trouble. Perhaps it was the presence of Miklos, by my side since we had left Crete that was keeping him away. (Except for last night in my hotel room, after I went inside to recover from the kisses, my mind reminded me.)

I had sent my wire to my father first thing, announcing that I would like to visit him, but he hadn't sent a reply. We had also visited a travel agency located not far from the hotel and reserved two rooms in Kymi for the night. We could have gone on traveling and caught the ferry to Skyros today, but Miklos encouraged me to rest and journey in steps. And, as part of me was reluctant to push myself into my father's arms, I didn't mind waiting another day.

Kymi was delightful to my eye. It had a Tyrolean feel, but saying that made Miklos ask many questions and demand that I pin down exactly what the reference meant. I just enjoyed the hillsides, some of them full of white buildings with red tile roofs. We arrived at our hotel and again there was an argument about who was paying. But I insisted. It seemed the least I could do, especially if he was the reason that I was no longer sighting that wretched man. Here I sent another wire, informing my father, if he was interested, that I was near and would be at the hotel for a full twenty-four hours. Miklos left me at my room door with my cases and said he'd see me at dinner.

Apparently he had a few friends here as well, and he was going to use the hotel lobby phone and try to get a hold of them. I sat on my twin bed in my room and sighed. I had a few hours to pass, but I felt no inclination to leave the hotel and wander the streets of Kymi by myself.

I remembered how that blond man had entered my room in Athens and shuddered. I got up and locked my door and the door to the balcony. I opened my cases and unpacked a few things for the evening. And then I settled back onto my bed with a good book.

Taking a nap felt wonderful. I woke up slowly to see the light in the room had darkened. It was disorienting. I sat up and turned on the bedside lamp, and saw that over four hours had passed. It was early evening now, the sun nearly spent. We had arranged to meet for dinner an hour and a half ago.

I swung my feet out of bed and scrambled for my sandals. I went to the mirror and brushed my hair back, examining my face. I was pink-cheeked from the nap, but otherwise presentable. Taking up my purse and my room key I ventured out into the hallway, assuming that Miklos must have fallen asleep like I had done. I went to his room door and knocked.

There was no answer, and the utter silence of the room on the other side of the door and the hallway finally began to alarm me.

"Miklos?" I called, knocking again. And then, taking courage into my hands, I opened the door to his room.

The inside shocked me. The room was in disarray, but not the kind of mess a person made when they were untidy or in a hurry. This was eerily like my room had been back in Athens; the bed toppers were pulled off onto the floor, a small table was knocked over, and his suitcase was open and spilling out its contents.

My stomach turned right over. I ran into the hallway, down to the lobby, and began squeaking to the attendant behind the counter.

His English was thick, but he understood that I was upset. I described my friend, pointed out that he had used the phone, and tried to tell him that I was afraid because he was missing. I mentioned the police, insisting that they be called right away. The fellow behind the counter nodded and went over to the phones. But he came back a moment later with a paper in his hand on which he had scrawled a few lines of numbers.

"What's this?" I demanded.

"Your friend," he said.

'What about him? Did he say he could be reached here? Are you telling me this is his number?"

"Your friend ... he call."

I sighed and resisted the temptation to pull my hair and screech. I merely handed him the paper and demanded that he make the connection for me. This seemed to please him, and he gestured with great courtesy over to the bank of public phones. Soon I had the receiver in my ear listening to the clicks of the phone service. I waited with a pounding heart for it to be answered on the other side, hoping against hope that Miklos could be found there. The phone was picked up and I jumped in eagerness.

"Yasa." I heard on the other end. The voice was deep, and male, but it wasn't Miklos. I scrambled for what he had taught me.

"Parakalo ... pou ine ... Miklos?"

The man on the line figured things out fast.

"Excuse me?" he asked in English. "You are looking for something?"

"Yes! Oh, thank you! I'm looking for Miklos! Miklos Iasonas! Do you know him?"

"Miklos, yes. I know him."

"Well, is he there?"

"No, not here. Yet. He comes to visit tonight. He brings a friend."

"I'm his friend. I'm Therese. I'm staying at the same hotel, but he didn't come to my room to pick me. He's late and I'm worried."

"Ah. But don't worry. We in Greece, we are late. Don't worry."

"But you don't understand," I shrieked, loud enough to freeze dust motes.

"Miss," he said after a moment of hesitation. "Is something wrong? You're frightened to be alone in Greece? But don't worry. People in Greece are very good to American tourists."

"Listen. Miklos wasn't in his room. I checked. And his bed was torn apart, and the furniture was knocked over, and his suitcase was gone through. Does that seem like nothing to worry about to you?"

The man was practical it seemed, and he was the sort that got things done.

"You're at the hotel Miklos mentioned? You stay, I come," he said, obviously ready to put down the phone.

"But wait. Who are you? And when will you come?"

"I am Andros. I'm the partner to Miklos. I'm here on business too, you understand?"

"But Andros, I remember you. From when we were children! You rowed the boat so Miklos could jump in and save me!"

A short chuckle.

"Yes, Therese. I remember you too. Now stay in hotel. I come right now. We find Miklos. Don't worry."

"Thank you. Efkharisto!"

We said goodbye and I laid down the receiver, before agitation made me move. I couldn't just stand here and do nothing. I pushed out the front door of the hotel and roamed up and down the street, realizing the pointlessness of that soon after. I charged back inside and demanded the police again, but the attendant only shook his head and pointed to the phones with a helpful smile. I stomped my foot and turned, charging back upstairs, to look first in my room and then in his. But nothing had changed.

It was a good thing that Kymi was a fairly small town. Just as I was about to plunge outside and find some shopkeeper who understood English better than the desk attendant so I could call the police, the outer door to the lobby opened and in came a young man, who was unmistakable. Unlike Miklos, Andros hadn't changed a bit. He looked just the same as he had at twelve, only he was taller and more filled out. I ran up to him, so disturbed now that tears left my eyes.

"Andros, what about Miklos? We have to call the police, but that man there won't understand me." I got out, my voice high with strain. I pointed to the offending desk clerk.

"Hello, Therese."

"Andros, please."

His eyes took in my state, and he went serious. He took my arm, so he could lead me over to the lobby couch and talk to me. But I tugged at him instead.

"Upstairs, Andros. Come and see for yourself."

He let me lead, and soon we were galloping up the stairs, to visit for the third time Miklos' room in its sad state of affairs. Andros entered the room and looked around, his face filling with disquiet.

But he shook his head, and I could tell that he thought the less sinister possibility to be the more likely one. So I took charge of the conversation once more.

"Andros, please sit and listen. There's a reason I'm so upset."

I lifted the chair from where it had fallen and led him over to sit on it. He allowed me, although he was a larger man even than Miklos. I sat on the bed opposite and leaned forward in earnest.

"One day back home in Seattle I was sitting alone in a waiting room," I began. "A strange man came in and stared at me. He had short blond hair that stuck up like bristles. He had pale blue eyes and scars on his chin and his cheeks. He had arms that were that thick." I tried to show him the width of the comic book muscles. "He said nothing, but I was beginning to fear him before he turned and left. I forgot all about him, until I flew here to visit Greece. That same man was on my plane. And at the airport he followed Miklos and me. Later on that day, Miklos had dropped me at my hotel and left me. I woke up from a nap, and that horrible man was in my room!"

Andros' eyebrows lifted, but he waited for me to go on.

"I slipped away from him and ran out, into the streets of Athens. When I lost him and returned, my room looked tossed just like this! He had gone through my things too. And the only thing he took from me was Miklos' letters. The ones I had saved and brought to show him."

"And you think this man came here today, from Athens?"

"There's more."

"More?"

"Yes. I saw that wretched man two more times! He came to Georgi's and Accalia's apartment the next morning. He shook me, and scared Accalia. And then, when we went to Crete, he came to the beach near the house of Miklos' parents. He came and grabbed me, but I got away."

Andros shook his head and then rubbed his face.

"All this, is true?"

"Yes."

"Then we go find Miklos."

He got up from his chair.

"You're going to call the police?"

He opened his mouth to reply, but at that moment a shadow

moved at the door. I screamed, a short burst of sound that cut off as soon as the man there stepped inside. He staggered a bit, and he had a bruise that reached from his cheekbone up against his right eye. But his eyes were clear.

"Miklos," I cried.

Chapter Fourteen

Soon we had Miklos sat down, and Andros went into the bathroom to soak a cloth for his eye. Miklos took the cloth from him in impatience. And then he did something that annoyed me. He reeled off and started talking in Greek to Andros. They spoke for several minutes, and I could tell Andros was getting the whole story. I stood and stared, my face settling into sternness and my hands on my hips. But then I got to thinking that in all probability Miklos had been put in danger because of my problem, so perhaps he had the right to express himself in his own language first. Silent, I let them talk, and went around tidying the room. I was sitting on the floor, my legs folded under me, packing his shirts down into his suitcase, when they turned and remembered me. I was upset, but seeing him so animated as he talked to Andros helped to reassure me that he was all right.

I made my decision then. I'd been wrong to drag Miklos into this. The room grew quiet for a moment, and I didn't look up. I was traumatized every time I pictured to myself the loss of Miklos, of him being hurt, or worse; his parents having to do without him, and Myron and Alceste losing the contented smiles on their faces. Whatever trouble I had somehow gotten tangled in, I had no right to risk him. Two pairs of men's legs stopped near me, but I wasn't ready to deal with it.

"Therese?"

I shook my head.

"You seem upset," Miklos pointed out.

"Upset?" I said, my voice rising. "Upset!"

"Therese, you're yelling."

"Miklos, what happened?"

"Oh that," he said, his voice casual. "I'll tell you. I went out for a while this afternoon. I had some business to complete, and Andros came up here for that purpose. I just needed to run a few errands, you see, and then I planned on taking him the paperwork tonight when we went to visit our friends."

"Paperwork?" the man didn't pick up on my tone.

"Oh yes. We were left some money, in an American's inheritance. Not much, but it was a kind gesture, and just because we had befriended the man during a difficult time in his life. We thought this might be the time to expand, because there's a good boat here we're looking at! We came here to ..."

He saw that I was glaring at him, and at last, he realized what I might be upset about.

"But you don't want to hear about that," he said.

"At some other time I'd like to hear about that, Miklos; sometime other than now. But hearing about that instead of hearing about the pertinent issue? No, I really don't care to hear about it at all!"

"Pertinent?" put in Andros from the side.

"Schetikos," Miklos supplied.

"It was that man again that was the cause, wasn't it?" I demanded. He nodded, his face stoic.

"Did you wake up from a nap and find him in your room?"

"No, that wasn't it. I was out, as I said. I came back to check on you. I saw him at your door. I had no idea that he must've come in here first and tossed my room, as you put it, until now. But there he was leaning against your door, listening. I wanted to go attack him, but then I had a better idea. If he went in your room, then I'd stop him. But if he left, I'd follow him!"

"You followed him?"

"Yes. He's thickheaded, I think. He never noticed me."

"Then why do you have that black eye?"

"That was someone else."

"Someone else? You mean there's more?"

"He went to a fancy boat, at the harbor. Nice yacht, with a lower cabin and a fast motor. So I climbed aboard and looked around. Two men found me, and I pretended I was anergos," he directed over the Andros, and "unemployed," he said to me.

"And these men beat you up?" I asked, my hand to my lips.

"Well, I wouldn't say they beat me up," he protested. "They just told me to stay away, and left me this." He pointed to the swollen part of his face. "As a reminder of what would happen if I returned. Anyway, your blond thug didn't know I was ever aboard."

"Those two might have reported you to him."

"Telling him what? That a Greek beggar came on board? He can't know it was me."

"And so what, anyway, Miklos? What did you learn?"

"I learned where he came from. And, I think I know where that boat is going next, also to Skyros! I saw some boxes in the cabin that had *Skyros* printed on the side."

"Oh, no."

I closed the lid of his suitcase and got up. I tried to think of what to do next, but thick thugs with mysterious yachts, peopled by guards who beat up defenseless unemployed Greeks? I had no idea how to deal with any of it. The police would take a report if I called them, and maybe put some clues together after a real crime happened to me, like kidnapping or death. Meanwhile, Miklos was getting more embroiled by the second, and was no doubt ready to bring in Andros as well. I turned dramatically toward the two men and stamped my foot.

"No," I insisted, trying to appear strong but sounding more like a duck missing the guttural in its quack. I was a squeak toy, colored bright but harmless. Miklos scratched the back of his head.

"No what?" he asked.

I took a deep breath.

"I want you to know how grateful I am," I began. "I wrote you all those years ago, and you must have thought I was strange. But you've been a friend to me, and a good one. But this is too much! What am I but a stranger that you're being kind to? I see now that you've grown up fine, that you're a good man from a great family. All that I hoped you would be. But we're not children anymore. I'm a woman too, grown and on my own now. There are two friends here, Miklos. You to me, and me to you. And that's why I say, as your friend, no."

He was glaring, and his voice simmered as he answered me.

"And I say, no what? What do you mean?"

"I mean that I want you to take this suitcase that I've packed up for you. I want you to go with Andros. Go to your friends and your paperwork and your new boat! I don't want your help anymore!

Whatever this is that's happening to me, I'm not a child and I'm not your little sister. I'll take care of it."

Now there were two handsome Greek statues staring at me. Emotion flared but I repressed it, trying to make a grand exit, instead of running out whining like I felt like doing. I shut the door on Miklos, right as he woke up to move toward me. His voice was cut off. Hurrying to my room I shoved and pushed my clothes and my passport and my toiletries in various carry-alls. I got right to the door dragging the load before he knocked. I opened it and ignored him, hefting my luggage, waddling by both men down the hallway. Miklos hurried beside me.

"Therese! What are you doing? Don't be like this. You can't run out into the night knowing nothing about the city. Where will you go? Andros and I, we can take you someplace safe, if you want to move."

I stood up and stopped the progression, breathing hard.

"I mean it, Miklos, leave me alone. Don't worry. You'll hear from me soon. I'll write to you, or even call you. But if something terrible happened to you because of me I'd never forgive myself! Now let me go, unless you intend to keep me prisoner."

"Can't we wait until you calm down and see sense instead?" he asked.

"You'll never want to make the break. You're just trying to put me off until I do things your way."

"Make the break?"

"Ooh! You can understand what I mean by that, can't you? No matter when I tell you no, you're not going to like it."

He walked up to me slowly. I let him, because I didn't want to hurt his feelings. Soon his two hands were holding mine, his warm and giving, and mine locked and ice cold.

"Listen please," he cajoled. "You're upset, and you were scared that I was missing. I'm sorry about that. I should've thought how you'd feel. But don't let that separate us right when you need my friendship the most. At least let Andros and I get you settled tonight. After that, if you want me to leave you, I will, if you insist. But if you run out this way, alone into Kymi where that man could find you, how do you expect me to be happy?"

"He has your address, Miklos. He has to see that I'm no longer with you. He has to realize that I left you and went out on my own.

That's the only way we can break this cycle of him following us."

"Or we could disappear tonight, together. Andros can help us. He can stay back on the highway and make certain we haven't been followed. We'll find a place, in fact I know of a little house that isn't being used right now. It's not a hotel, or a holiday rental. From there we can look up your father, and maybe he can tell you what this is all about."

I had pulled my hands from his as he tried to persuade me, and I stood twisting them. The fear that I had been putting to the side made me start shaking. My home address was known, as well as Miklos. His parent's house was known. But staying in public places and those familiar landmarks was inviting the touch of that stubby-haired rodent that was pestering me.

All of a sudden I was wheezing, and my breath tangled into a spasm. I was coughing, the fit taking over while I bent my shoulders and covered my mouth with my hands.

And then I was in Miklos' arms. He encircled me lightly, rubbing my back.

"Shhh," he whispered, adding a few sentences in Greek in a voice that would have tempted children to visit Hamlin. "We'll hide, Therese. We'll go where he can't find us. Until you feel stronger. Say yes," he urged, and I closed my eyes. The spasm began to leave and I opened my eyes to see Andros, standing a few feet away as a witness. If there had been any censure toward me in his gaze I would've said no. But there was only concern, and the expression on his face was so exactly the same as it had been twelve years ago when Miklos pulled me out of the water that I was struck by the memory.

How had it happened that in living a free and easy life with my mother, which embodied no attachments and no responsibilities, that I'd found a family here? I shook my head in defeat, and trusted to hope, and to Miklos' cleverness and his superior knowledge of his own country.

"All right," I said, my voice small. "But please, Miklos, hide us well."

Chapter Fifteen

Of course we didn't go right away to hide that evening. We had to go and tell his friends. They'd made a special dinner in our honor. This time I held back on too much wine. I absorbed the people instead. Their warmth and their contentment took my chill away. Their laughter and the light in their eyes made me happy to be sitting there among them. Miklos was right to make time for this. By the time the evening was done and it was late, I felt like his friends were my friends. And then we departed, with many handshakes and several people kissing me on the cheek.

I knew that Miklos and Andros had spent time telling several of the men my business. I'd seen them talking; heads bent and faces earnest with the serious. Could it be that they weren't as terrorized as I was by the pursuit of that stubby-haired threat? Did they think they could devise a plan for dealing with that shadowy figure?

It seemed that they did. Miklos told me all about it while we were driving. Andros followed behind us on a motorcycle, and our friend Matthaios drove us.

"We need to do some investigating," Miklos said. "We know where that man went. We can find out who owns the boat and try to discover their business. Meanwhile our friends will come and tell us what they've found, and they'll bring us food and send your messages. You need to send your father another wire, and have him respond to you at the hotel. Our friends will pick up the messages there for us."

"Miklos, I don't know what to say. Will our friends be safe?"

"Of course," he bellowed with ease. I thought perhaps it was the wine talking, but it was nice to see such confidence.

"And then?"

"We must go after this man, Therese. It's better than sitting and waiting for him to come after us."

"But he might be more dangerous than we suspect."

"Is he an army?"

I smiled and shook my head.

"You're afraid of him, and that's natural," he assured me. "But you're not alone now."

I suspected that he thought I'd been afraid just because I was a woman, and I felt a little ruffled. After all, anyone with sense would be afraid of a man who looked like he lifted two hundred pound barbells for fun every morning before breakfast. But I didn't say anything. I'd be a fool to resist this group of men and their plans. If I wanted to keep Miklos safe as well as myself, it behooved me to use every advantage possible. And the fact that all of these men seemed to be having a good time, that this troublesome enemy needed to be stopped and they were the boys to do it, was a mystery that perhaps showed up one of the differences between our genders. Miklos went on talking, telling me which of his friends was going to do what. I was pleased that I remembered all of their names.

After a while we slowed, and Miklos pointed out that behind us Andros was pulling off to the side of the road to hide next to an old square building. It was a good place for him to watch the road, and make certain that no one was following us. What he was supposed to do if he did notice a car behind us I wasn't certain. I only hoped that he didn't plan on confronting Mr. Block-arms himself.

We waved at him and picked up speed again, and I rested against the seat. I was alone in the back of the car, and I appreciated it. Here the night lowered, now that Miklos had stopped talking. We'd left the city limits of Kymi a while ago, and the road twisted, and yet the stars were visible through the front windshield and out my window.

The drive took on a quality that put me in the same mind as the group of men I'd been questioning a moment before. There was something about danger being forced on you, and relying on your intelligence and your friends to pull you out of it. The dark road was leading to a land of adventure, a hidden cottage made for refugees and stowaways. The stark yet beautiful landscape, dim out of range of the car's headlights, was founded with stone, ageless and used to the tempestuous footprints of Grecian history. This land held firm, it persevered, and its people faced difficulties head on. Whether or not all of this was wise, I couldn't question.

A part of me missed home now, my life back in Seattle. I missed my little kitchen. I missed the cans of soup on the shelf and the package of Malamars in the pantry. I missed my bed with its flowered quilt. I'd bought some cheerful rugs for my bedroom, in a gold and white striped pattern. I'd put Holly Hobbie café curtains up, just because I liked the colors and the printed pattern against the light blue walls. It was a room to please a high school girl, for at twenty-two, I wasn't afraid to admit to myself that it was nice to have a place where my childhood still lingered. When I went back, and made that house my own, when it was the home of a trendy young woman of the seventies, I could move into my mother's empty bedroom and decorate like a grown-up.

I allowed my dreams of an easier life to placate me for a time, but then my gaze traveled over to Miklos, talking quietly in Greek to his friend. His eyes were focused straight-ahead, intent on the road. He'd told me that the little house was off the main byway, and up a narrow track. He'd never been there, for it was a house that belonged to the cousin's parents of a friend that lived not in Kymi, but in Athens. He'd called his friend sometime during dinner, and I'd offered to pay the phone charge. Yes, of course we could use the house. However, there was no key, cold water only, barren shelves, cooking by use of the molded stone fireplace, and the electricity, never certain, had been shut off for good measure. Once Miklos had reported this to his posse of eager deputies, a collection had been taken up. Nearby neighbors were called, despite the hour. Supply offerings were hand delivered. Spates of rapid Greek were spoken and quick introductions were made. I suspected that my business would soon be broadcasted by mouth until it reached Crete to disturb Miklos' family. It was a good thing that he'd called them already. He told me he was talking to Myron.

I'd let all the words I didn't understand wash over me during the evening. Even if the whole city soon knew that Miklos and Andros, friends to so and so, were helping a defenseless American girl escape from an assailant twice her size who had attacked her more than once, somehow I didn't doubt that the loyal cleverness of these people would make certain that no glimmer of gossip reached the ears of those brutes on the fancy boat.

I told myself that this experience was rare. Perhaps I wasn't cocooned in my girl's bedroom back home, under the covers with a good book. But here I was being cocooned in a different way, wrapped in the good will of strangers.

All of the sudden the car took a turn, due to an exclamation from Miklos. I sat up and tried to see. If this was a track I didn't know how it stood out. Two twin lines, pencil thick against the parchment of rugged green. We bumped and vibrated up a hill, and then blended behind the hillside. We were out of sight of the road. The track leveled out and a hulking shape appeared before us. The house was a dried out rectangle, with a slope roof of old tile. Its smooth outer layer was in sad need of whitewash. But there were square windows that peeped at us, like shy peasants. The door was short; Miklos would have to stoop. It was made of wide planks of wood. I got out of the car and wrapped my thin button-up sweater tighter over my middle. Somewhere in the vastness behind the house, I could hear the sea. The men had opened the trunk of the car and were taking out a few boxes. I hurried to help, grabbing up some thick blankets that we'd borrowed from what neighbor I couldn't guess. Miklos strode up and opened the front door, taking, a moment later, the lantern that Matthaios had just lit. They went inside to illuminate the windows.

I followed with my blankets. The interior was bare, but there was an old scrubbed wooden table in the kitchen, a lone chair by the back door, and a carved wooden bench against the far wall. Another chair stood, for some unknown reason, in the middle of the room. For it was a one-room house in many ways. Except I could see a tiny bathroom, and two doors along the darkened back wall. I liked the place at once. While I stood looking around the men had been going in and out, bringing in the supplies.

A box of food, put together in a hurry and filled with undiscovered contents. A few thin pillows, and more blankets clean but rubbed thin with use, some towels, a box of utensils and kitchen implements, candles, matches, soap, and a broom that looked like a witch's ride. Three cups, three plates, three bowls; and even, from some thoughtful soul, a cookbook. I stood the whole time they busied themselves holding my blankets, thankful of them now. And when they were done, Miklos held out a hand and Matthaios shook it. I broke my long silence and held out my hand too, and Matthaios shook it more gingerly.

"Thank you," I said to him, my voice sounding tired. "Please tell Andros to let everyone know how much I'm thankful for all of their help. And please ask all your friends to be careful. I don't want anyone hurt because of me. Tell him to say how sorry I am to cause so much trouble."

The man smiled and looked over to Miklos, who translated the finer points.

"No, no," the fellow said. "I'll return soon."

Miklos and I stood in the doorway and watched him turn the car around and drive off.

"He'll go back and talk to Andros where he's watching the road," Miklos told me. "That way there won't be any doubt. If we were followed, Andros would've seen it by now. Then Matthaios will come back and stay with us tonight, and perhaps tomorrow night as well."

To be a chaperone, I wondered? Or was he returning to help Miklos in some way I hadn't heard about? I shook my head.

"That's quite an efficient team you've drummed up," I said.

He grinned.

"'Drummed up?'"

"Pulled out of your hat? Whisked together?"

"Now you're teasing me."

"I hope Andros gets home all right."

"Of course he will. If Andros thought someone suspicious was following, he would've come here to help us. Don't worry. Now come, let's find out where we'll be sleeping."

Chapter Sixteen

The next few days in the simple house passed quietly, and yet I knew that the memory of them would bring peace to my mind for the rest of my life. In the hot part of the day Miklos and I were most often alone, for Matthaios left to go to work and to retrieve messages in Kymi each day.

Meanwhile I awoke to the sun, spilling in the tiny window of the larger bedroom each morning, nestled in a pile of blankets on the stone floor. There was nothing else in my room but cheerful dust motes and forgotten memories. I would lay and stare at the ceiling and wonder who had lived here, and what their lives had been like. Had they raised children here? Did they keep livestock in the little outbuilding by the edge of the track, or see by candlelight as we did each night?

The second day in, there was a lot of laughter early that morning, for Matthaios had gone shopping for me, and I was trying to make use of what he had been able to understand from my list. First it had been my task to get him to agree to keep the change from the money I'd given him. Then Miklos had come out, stretching his shoulders and nodding at Matthaios' chopped English and my few words of Greek. I had the flat pot over the fire, and was trying to get the butter to sizzle right.

"What is this glitsa avgo?" Matthaios said, turning halfway to Miklos. I could see by the light in the men's eyes that they were teasing me.

"Glit-za avgo?" I asked.

"Slimy eggs," Miklos supplied with a grin.

"You've seen eggs and milk before, I know!"

"Yes, but when you make them it seems more slimy."

"You just wait! American toast is my specialty!"

"Not French toast?"

"Yes, but my mother and I modified it."

Miklos held up the jar of honey that had been bought.

"I see. So that's what this is for? To cover the taste?"

I threatened to kick them out of the kitchen, but as they were dealing with the heavy pot and there was nowhere else to go, the threat was empty. A few minutes later I pointed out that they were eating all the toast despite their complaints. In fact, soon it was all gone, most of a loaf of bread and half of the jar of honey. Matthaios was cheerful as he set off for work.

"Perhaps your father, he call today!" he said, trying to keep my spirits up. I nodded and smiled; for 'call' was the only way he knew how to say, send you a wire.

Getting the dishes cleaned was another challenge in the cold water, as well as us. I was thankful that the family of whoever inherited this house had decided to modernize the plumbing and put in a toilet, back when they thought they could sell the place.

The long days, healed by the heat and the solitary beach at the foot of the steep hillside, I seemed to spend most of my time in my comfortable sundress and my red swimsuit. Taking the oldest blanket down with me, laying it on the near-white rock silt of beach, reading and sleeping until Miklos joined me.

But he was what made it golden. We didn't talk all the time, but that smile of his was becoming more attractive to me all the time. His gentle hands were often clamped in mine, for I couldn't seem to stop myself from making use of the contact. The lean firmness of his fingers threaded through mine as we sat side by side looking out over the water was a simple joy like all the rest.

One time, we even necked. It seemed like such a natural development, for we were very close to each other, lying on the blanket. I was on my stomach with one leg bent up, and he was on his side. My head was turned sideways as we chatted, and then I rolled to face him. The next thing he had bent his head down, and I had risen to meet his kiss. I didn't feel like a teenager, having my first real fling with romance. I didn't feel like a sensual woman either. It was just part of it, blended with the clean sun and the kindness of the man beside me. It wasn't a moment of passion, but of a deeper knowledge of each other beyond words. For several minutes his lips explored mine, and the deep silence of his concentration filled the deserted landscape and made us seem like the only two people in the world.

And then, whether it was because he was content, or because I was a girl he was helping and it wasn't right to have too much fun doing it, he sat up and helped me move beyond the moment by giving me that smile.

"Stay here and rest, Pouli," he said. "I'll go get us some lunch."

He came back with a basket twenty minutes later, filled with olives, feta cheese, stiff bread, and golden wine. We ate and watched the sea birds, and talked about our days in college, comparing the differences between his night school in Heraklion and my sojourn at the University of Washington.

"You'd think with an Education degree you could learn to speak more Greek," he said.

"You want me to get to know more Greeks?"

"You can only attract so many, Pouli. Not enough fancy feathers."

"What's wrong with what I have on?"

His eyes danced.

"I remember you having more than one swimsuit. Didn't your mother send you another one? If you went and tried that little yellow thing on, I could tell you if it's okay."

It was cute when he said the word okay.

"Hey man, I'm just holding that for my mother!"

"'Hey man,'" he teased, like he always did when I used slang.

"Besides," I added, "that bikini wouldn't keep me very warm!"

"You're right," he agreed, pulling me close to his side. "And I guess that little suit might attract too many Greeks. You stay like you are."

I determined each morning not to jump off the cliff into headlong love. I still had no real idea if Miklos was going to jump off with me. Perhaps he was just being a friend, and holding hands and kissing a willing American seemed like nothing much to him. I was old enough to desire my dignity, but not mature with men enough to be able to read him. Nevertheless I allowed myself the pleasure of being aware of romance, blossoming beside me like a secret companion. One of the things that helped settle my happiness was the certainty that I was safe. I knew that blond villain couldn't find me. A different friend of Matthaios went into my hotel each day at a different time to retrieve any messages and to send the belated letter to my mother that I took the time to write. One of the desk clerks was another friend, and we could be sure that no one would be given information from him. I even had the messenger cancel my reservation in Crete that Xavier had made for me before I left Seattle. Wherever I stayed in Greece from now on, it wouldn't be from a pre-planned itinerary.

On the evening of the third day two cars arrived, full of the friends I had made from Kymi before I came out here with Miklos. Again, Andros had pulled up to hide on the road behind them, and was waiting for a quarter of an hour to make certain that no car followed before he joined us, riding his motorcycle up the tiny track that wrapped behind the hillside.

I laughed with delight when the car doors opened, for the whole crew was there. Out of the second car eight people disentangled themselves, and among them, like a present, was both Accalia and Alceste, and their husbands. Miklos was just as happy to see them as I was. Myron greeted him with a handshake and a masculine kiss on one cheek.

"You don't look like a man hiding away from a dangerous gang to me, brother!" he laughed, and the crowd crowed, spilling sentences in Greek that must be about the challenges of hiding out with a pretty girl, for Miklos got red and pushed them all away. Then someone caught me into a hug, and we all entered the tiny rectangle house. Dinner had been brought with them, and the big fireplace was lit up. Extra plates were pulled out of their packets for the occasion, and I suggested having an American picnic since the table was too small to seat sixteen.

"Picnic!" several of them said as I finished sweeping with my witch's broom and laid out a thick blanket as a table on the floor. They seemed to like the word.

I encouraged them to talk in Greek as we shared the food. Sitting on the floor, the girls' legs curled under them, the candles leaning and sputtering on the bumpy blanket, I was happy to hear the cadence of their talk. It struck me that it didn't matter where a person lived in the world, because sixteen young people can enjoy being together in a way that changed things. None of us here would drop out, or fade from existence. With so much connection, anything was possible.

I had stopped looking at my watch days ago, but I knew it must be after midnight before the cars loaded up again. Andros was staying over with us, for he and Miklos had business to discuss in the morning. Myron and Alceste were going to go back to Crete tomorrow, for they had just come to check on family. They all were taken in as guests in the easy, free-flowing hospitality of the people in Kymi. I decided not to feel guilty about putting this great number of people to so much trouble. They were so obvious in their enjoyment. It wasn't until the cars were started and we had waved and said our goodbyes that Matthaios came up to Miklos and me where we stood beside the track.

The car tires crunched and they rounded the hill and disappeared.

"Ah, Therese," Matthaios said, pausing to yawn. He dug in his pocket and pulled out a golden-orange folded paper square. "You got a message today at the hotel," he went on, handing it to me. "From your father."

Chapter Seventeen

The candlelight flickered over the crinkled paper, making the fact that my fingers were shaking less noticeable. I'd been jittery ever since the telegram had been placed in my hand. My father had sent a message to me for the first time in my life. He hadn't seen my mother pregnant or visited me as a newborn. Had he felt irritated when he heard the news that he was a father? Or did he feel nothing at all?

The dinner in my stomach wasn't welcome. The four of us were at the table, which we had pulled over to be used near the bench. They were in their corners and I was alone at mine. The three men sitting on the other side of the candle sat back in the shadows and said nothing. I couldn't see their faces lit up. And in fact, I was alone in this. My first moment with my father was something no one else could understand. I set my fingers in the crease, tore the telegram open, and read it.

MAY, 1975

THERESE LINDSEY... STOP... GOT YOUR TELEGRAM... STOP ...COME TO ME HERE SO WE CAN MEET ... STOP... I HAVE SOMETHING TO SHOW YOU... STOP.
AUSTIN FROMME, YOUR FATHER ... STOP

I held the paper up in disappointment, turning it over even though I knew that was all. How easy it would be to just lower it now, into the flame of the candle. There was an address listed for me to come to, and it was the same as the address on my mother's letter. It wasn't Skyros, but an island nearby. An island so small that it had few inhabitants to speak of, and no large port either. It was called Patismasia, which Miklos had told me meant "footprint."

I lifted the paper, allowing it to survive, up and over the candle flame, and Miklos took it. He and Matthaios and Andros read it together. Matthaios murmured a question; Miklos translated a word for him. But their conversation was as short as the telegram. I smiled, but felt tragic.

"Not much written on that paper to encourage me to visit is there?" I said.

Matthaios murmured.

"Entharryno," Miklos said to him.

I wondered if he could translate my feelings for me as easy as he translated English for his friends. I blinked, allowed a tear to fall, sniffed hard and refused anymore.

I didn't know what I was grieving for, except the absence of anything worth grief. The paper was handed back to me, and I laid it on the table. I pressed it out flat. I folded along the original seams. Then I looked up. Miklos was leaning forward now, and I let him into my gaze for a short second.

"I'm going to take a walk," I announced. His eyebrow lifted but he didn't protest.

The next thing I was hurrying, snatching my sweater from a hook by the door. Soon I was outside, glancing back and seeing the open doorway with two men standing in it. The sight made me hurry more. This was my life, and my need to be alone; my choice to fly if I felt restless, and my mistake if I took a spill. I didn't go down to the water, or around the hillside on the little track. I pushed the other way, uphill and over the rough terrain. The stumpy grass was lush with plant life I wasn't familiar with in the dark. The moon was thin; nearly at it's least. The stars were distant and piercing, making the sky a glowing tapestry but giving no light to my feet. The hill grew steep and I tripped on a white rock, hidden like the half-hump of an Easter egg in the grass. A bush scratched at me, but I kept going. The challenge of the hillside was comforting in its meaninglessness. This too set me apart. Perhaps I wasn't the only girl ever to scramble up this hill, while wondering if her stay here was temporary. How long till she was forgotten, like the other girls in the distant past who had claimed this path?

At last I stopped and sat, on a near-flat rock that stood out like a bald spot. I pulled my knees up and wrapped my arms around them. I put my head in the pocket.

I could see it now like never before; here in a country that cherished family, how important it was to have parents who loved you. Whether or not you had outlived them, to know that you had mattered, to someone, very much. With that knowledge you were grounded. Like a good investment, it was an asset you could always fall back on. And now I admitted it to myself. Even though I knew June loved me, I'd wanted more. My father had been an unknown before, but that telegram was sneering at me that he didn't care and never would. I didn't want him to show me something. I wanted him to look up, to see me as something special.

I didn't bother crying. I just sat and felt small, and then I let the rareness of that hillside absorb into me. I was in Greece, on the other side of the globe from Seattle, with dust instead of damp under the grass and segments of history written in ruins. Here the sun brought out the true colors. And here I would find out what the definition of my past was and what I intended to do about it.

Of course Miklos had to find me in the end. I wasn't moving from that spot till the cold or another impetus broke my concentration. The flashlight he was carrying flickered over the hillside, announcing his presence. It took a full ten seconds for me to land back on Earth, and to escape the lofty introspective world I'd been locked in. By the time he appeared, standing over me with a serious look on his face I frowned at him.

"Do you mean to tell me that I've been wandering around that little house in the middle of the night when I needed to visit the bathroom with my hands in front of me like a blind woman, when all the time you've had that flashlight with you?" I demanded.

He stiffened at the accusation, and then he chuckled. He folded, and sat next to me on the bald spot.

"Forgive me, but I don't think of you wandering the little house in the middle of the night," he replied. "I go into the room and sleep."

I shook my head.

"You didn't have enough sisters," I told him.

"I've had plenty of cousins and aunts and a mother."

"True. I hope you're grateful."

"I am. Don't be so forlorn, Pouli. It hurts me."

"If you didn't want to see a woman feel sorry for herself, what'd you come up here for?"

"Maybe I wondered what it would be like to kiss you on top of this hillside with nothing but the stars to see us."

He startled me.

"What?" I gasped.

He'd talked about it. He'd admitted that he wanted to kiss me, and that it took over his thoughts.

"Don't look so scared," he said, looking disgruntled.

"Scared isn't the word to describe what I'm feeling."

"What is that word then?"

I sighed and looked out at the depths.

"I wasn't in the mood to describe anything. I came up here to feel, to let emotion have its way with me. Go away, Miklos."

"While you wait until emotion is done with you before coming back down? I'd never see you again."

Now I chuckled.

"Go away," I commanded again.

"No."

I nudged him.

"Great strong man with a flashlight," I said. "Leave the hillside to the blind woman."

He nudged me back. I pushed and he responded. Soon it was back and forth, and a wrestling match went on until I fell over, onto my back and he tipped over me. It was a classic stance, seen on every daytime drama and Burt Lancaster film that ever graced the two-in-the-morning movie on our TV set back home. I was supposed to freeze under his arms, and look up at him with doe eyes.

"Where's that chaperone when I need one?" I whispered.

His grin looked wicked.

"I told Matthaios and Andros to go on to bed."

"If you kiss me now," I told him, "you'll wonder if it was me or emotion kissing you back."

"I didn't climb up here to take advantage of you in these weeds."

"That's just an added bonus?"

He laughed and got off me. Soon we were sitting back on the bald spot. The silence settled, but it wasn't charged with power like it had been when I was alone. Now it offered a different type of magic, but as the cold began to seep in I yawned. Magic was just too much bother. I leaned against him and yawned again.

"No, Pouli, don't sleep here."

"I'm tired."

"Well let's go back then."

"I want a piggy back ride."

"What do you think I am?"

"Bernie the taxi-cab driver?"

He stood up and took hold of my hands, pulled me to my feet and turned on the flashlight. He nestled it into the crook of one elbow while he tucked my hand in the crook of his other arm.

"How's this?"

"Mmm. Nice."

The walk down was slow, too careful, but I felt like I was going down the elevator back into normalcy. The rectangle of the little house appeared in the clearing, and I took a deep breath. It was going to be all right, as long as I could hold off any further attacks by stubby-haired, comic book thugs, that is. At the door I stopped us, pulling out my arm to face him. I got on my tiptoes and kissed his cheek.

"Thank you, Miklos," I breathed.

"For what?"

"For making me feel wanted, and then not doing anything about it."

I turned and went in before he could say anything, holding out my hands in the darkened interior. But he reached out and took hold of my elbow. His warm hand lowered down my arm till it reached my fingers. And then his flashlight was placed in my grip. Emotion tipped its hat, for a last fling, but I ignored it. I just wanted to visit the bathroom, so I could stumble to my room, get nested into the blankets and sleep.

Chapter Eighteen

Miklos and I got on the ferry to Skyros, and just like that, my blond, stubby-haired nemesis was back on my trail. But I didn't know it until we were leaving the ferry, and I was admiring the sparkling sun on the dark turquoise blue water in the main port town of the island, Linaria. We were at the bottom of the stairs, and before us was the edge of the ferry where the cars drove off. I turned to catch a glimpse of Skyros, and there, in the line of people leaving the ferry behind me, I saw the man, tucked high in the far corner at the end of the line.

Numbness came over my emotions, and I picked him out with my eyes. I was the one observing him now, staring at his features and the details of his life at that moment, without him knowing of my scrutiny. It was a sight I didn't desire. If Miklos hadn't been there, standing to the side of the line a little ahead of me arranging straps on his shoulder and preparing to carry too much luggage, I would've darted away. I would've slipped behind a pillar or post, waited until my quarry had gotten in front, and then followed him. But as it was I touched Miklos' arm, and when he looked up I pointed, and let the crestfallen expression on my face do the rest.

His mind worked quickly. He turned, but he couldn't see the fellow from where he was standing. Any moment the line would move forward and we would be in the fellow's sight range. Both of us, with our eyes connected, received the same order to action at the same moment. I snatched a suitcase, and Miklos took my arm. And then we were crouching, taking the course away from the line of debarking travelers. We curved behind the line of vehicles on the ferry, still bent double. We settled in behind a truck, it's bed filled with uneven crates.

From there we saw it all. Stubbo placid as he moved down

the stairs and left the gangplank, his head lifting to find us in the crowd, and his shoulders tensing slightly when he couldn't spot us. We saw him increase his speed, try to push past the people in front of him. We saw his head craning around, and we both ducked instinctively when his gaze scanned in our direction. But when we peeked again it was all right. He was going to run for it, and find us up ahead in the streets of Linaria. We saw his hands pushing through people like he was paddling through the sea. And then the irritated shoulders of the inconvenienced travelers, who were unaware of what a true nuisance the man was, closed back in the gap and sealed him off from our view. I dropped the suitcase, which I had been clutching to my chest without being aware of it, at my feet. Then I buried my head in my hands.

And Miklos, dropping his own cases, yanked me into his arms. Numbness had faded now. I could feel myself shaking.

"Shhh," he said.

"Miklos, let's stay on the ferry," I whispered. "I don't want to go this way. Not with him here."

He was holding me close, kissing my head, and then my eyebrows, and then the tears on my cheeks. I opened my mouth to complain about his timing, and was caught up in a kiss so fierce that we were both shaking together. He cradled my skull with his lean hands, and I helped, molding our lips, gasping for breath, and finding his kiss again. I broke the contact with a loud smack.

"Let's go back," I wheezed again.

"Yes," he hissed in breathless reply. He picked up the cases. "Back into the main cabin of the ferry."

"Yes," I agreed.

Then we were scurrying, into the depths of the ferry. We sat backward at a table near the window. The ferry was empty of passengers, for the ones about to embark hadn't got on yet. We looked at the dock as best we could, hoping somehow for a glimpse of the awful person, so we could relax that we had left him behind. But of course we couldn't see him from here.

The minutes before the ferry was ready to leave again dragged. The deserted ferry ticked, settling into the water, taking its time. And then it nudged, just a little as the weight of first one car and then another began to drive on and park tight in their lines. At last there were new people, ambling, eyes distant in that gaze travelers use. Miklos and I said nothing. But we sat together, and I clutched his hand. When the ferry at last finished loading, rumbled up its engines and set off in a deep plow into the water, I had to unclench my muscles. Miklos scrambled to his feet.

"Stay here with the cases," he said, his accent thick. Then he left me, striding down the interior room of the ferry, his eyes roaming from side to side. I didn't have to wonder what he was doing. I knew he was searching, determined to spy every inch of the ferry, and prove that the blond man hadn't rejoined us. While he was gone I sat tense, staring out the window without seeing anything. I tried to think of what to do. Should I go somewhere out of the country, now while I was in the lead and couldn't be discovered? Should I take my father's money, spend it on a vacation selected at random, and disappear into the hidden fabric of the world where I couldn't be found? Perhaps I could go to Europe, or Africa. I could travel around for months until I was certain that whoever was following me had given up. And then I could go home. It would be better, I thought, than having my every moment in Greece destroyed by this virus of a person intent on bothering me. It would be preferable to risking Miklos.

I was a free woman. I had my passport. I could be safe. I could leave.

But all of these thoughts turned into wisps as I saw Miklos reappear and walk toward me, his eyes roaming one last time either side to be sure. If I left Greece I would have to leave him. By the time he came up to me and sat across on the seat opposite my face was serious and intent. He leaned forward and took my two hands.

"It's all right, Pouli," he said. "I walked the whole boat and looked into all the rooms. Unless he's staying with the Captain, he didn't get back on board with us."

I relaxed, but not all the way.

"Something has to change, Miklos," I said.

"I can tell you mean something by that."

"Yes, I do. This is insane! I just avoided that worm's grasp, again! How many more times until he catches me? And how fair is it for me to put you in harm's way?"

"Humph. I will harm him!"

I shook my head.

"If he were in a Popeye cartoon his muscles would look like two cement blocks."

"Ah, yes. Popeye I know."

"No can of spinach is going to make your fists tornados," I went on.

"And no brute is going to make you tall like Olive Oil, eh, Pouli?"

"Miklos this isn't funny. I have to do something."

His eyes were bright.

"Else," I added. "I have to do something else. Something unexpected. I can't appear on public transportation, or stay in any hotels. I have to leave Greece."

"But then you can't see your father!"

"I can't see him anyway. Not without risking too much."

"Yes, you can. I'll help you."

"Miklos, it isn't worth it. I can leave and then contact my father later. You'll be safe. I should do what's best."

He sat forward. His eyes shone with eagerness.

"Andros and me," he said. "We bought the boat!"

"You bought the boat?"

"Yes, and she's fine. She can go between Kymi and Skyros, and the other island your father is on. You'll be our first passenger! Stubbo can't find you then."

"Oh, but …"

My eyes panned over him. The brown skin at the base of his neck, the strong chin that had a dusting of beard growth. The straight nose, and the eyes that so captivated me. His hair was soft and wiry at the same time, joyful and strong. He looked so good I wanted to taste him, and I bit my lip.

"I really want to go with you," I said, and my eyes carried a double meaning.

If I thought he might flinch at that, I was wrong. He brought his gaze closer, and I saw in his face even more intensity and desire than I had.

"Then come with me," he answered.

It was a good thing we were on a ferry, in public, in the daytime. Otherwise I would've pretended that caviar was a monster plate full of spaghetti and indulged my appetite with giant bites of sensation. I wanted to kiss him again. My expensive tastes were making demands.

He isn't food, I told myself. *He's more than just delicious.*

He was staring back at me, and the crease at the side of his mouth was uptilted.

"What are you thinking about, little Pouli," he murmured.

I swallowed and breathed some sanity back into my system.

"I'm thinking that we need to have more help from your friends."

"More help? What were you thinking?"

"I was thinking we need a chaperone. Just look at you! Are you trying to take advantage of a poor American girl, alone in a strange country, sick too, I might add, that's confused and vulnerable and ready to cling to any man that seems to be her rescuer?"

He grinned.

"You can trust me, Pouli," was all he said.

I took his hands and pulled him over to sit next to me, so I could lean into his warmth. He wrapped his arm around my shoulder and obliged as I reached for his other hand. Back we went to Kymi.

Chapter Nineteen

I was nabbed on the other side. Kymi, built on a hill in Tyrolean majesty, filled with friends of friends of Miklos; yesterday it had networked together to hide me and provide for me. But in reality it was all a trap, and I had been circling it; eluding a few tricks and puzzles, but in the end, I was a mouse running through a maze to its inevitable finish.

We had exited the ferry, and Miklos had stepped away for a few moments. He was visiting the bank of phones around the corner. I was waiting with the cases. I was thinking that I had stepped back and was letting him plan everything, and wondering if that was all right for a young trendy girl of the seventies. But then all choice of what I could do next was taken from me. A shadow of two men stepped up behind me, and something cold and hard was pushed into my back. A man spoke in my ear, his breath on my neck.

"Miss Lindsey," he said. "You'll come with us."

I jumped and wrenched around, but they didn't let me go far. My upper arm was taken in a grip like a steel clamp, but I had the chance to see their faces. The accent the man spoke in was not Greek. They both had dark hair. They were both under forty. They were both fit and firm, and they neither one had any sympathy in their gazes. I opened my mouth to scream and the main speaker talked fast.

"It would be a shame to have to shoot your boyfriend if he came running," he said.

The threat was simple, but effective. A stern arm wrapped behind me, propelling me away from safety. I stumbled along, fear coursing up from my stomach, afraid to go with these men, and afraid to scream for help. The bright sunshine of Greece was stale now, unable to dazzle. Just like in the movies they took me right to a waiting car. The door was pushed open for me. I had my purse, but everything else had been left behind me. I imagined Miklos, for a moment, returning to the forlorn cases, searching, calling for me, and asking strangers if they saw anything. But soon my mind returned to my own problems.

"What do you want? Why have you taken me?" I gasped as we all got into the car and shut doors.

"Be quiet," the man said.

He had gotten behind the wheel, but his twin was in the back seat next to me. The front seat sent the back seat a glance. The fellow beside me reacted by hurting me. It wasn't glamorous like on TV. There wasn't a trim backhand applied leaving a genteel bruise. He merely turned in the seat, took up my hand and my wrist, and bent them back until I was up in the air, trying to relieve the strain. The more I pushed him, the harder he pressed. Then, with a twist that hurt in another way, he shoved me back to the seat and let me go. He crouched over me, his hand pressing now against my mouth, blocking also my nose and my ability to breathe. He kept forcing me back, bending my head, grinding deeper until my lips flattened against my teeth and my nose became moist. Then he squeezed in my cheeks with pincer fingers, so that my face had lost its features, and I was humiliated. Then he wiped his hand on his jacket with a look of disgust.

"Shut up," the fellow said.

He was disrespectful when he pulled back. He insulted me, a swearword that I had read in books but had never heard spoken aloud. I stayed in the corner. My hand, without thought, grabbed the door handle and pulled, but it had been disconnected. It didn't open from the inside. Now the man produced a backhand, and it was so fierce that my head was thrown all the way to the side and it made contact with the metal frame of the window.

I got the message. Don't talk or object in any way. I held up both hands in the traditional attitude of surrender. My face felt thick where he had struck me, and it was vibrating, not painful yet, but swelling. He stared forward, adjusting his shirt and looking out the window. The driver had been calm all throughout my instruction. A silence fell in the car now, and I was hyper-aware of myself. My breath was loud. I was sure that every time I swallowed it was filling the man beside me with disgust. The car ride didn't last very long. We circled the harbor. We drove to a smaller dock. We parked in the lot, and the bully beside me took a firm hold as the driver opened my door. Just to show me that there wasn't a chance that man hooked on to my other arm. I was dragged along between them, my two arms held so tight my shoulders were hunching.

I wondered why the world seemed suddenly empty. It was the early afternoon; surely there must be someone about? I could see a few humans further down, entering the streets of town, puttering in the back of their boats, looking bored and busy. But none were the sort that I could call to and get help. Against the dock was a boat, enclosed with a powerful motor. I was pushed into the cabin and forced to sit on a slippery wooden box at the back. The two men stood at the windows in front of the steering wheel like men do, owning the deck, creating the speed and the lift. The boat pulled away, and soared from the edge of the water, the wooden dock of all that I knew, and the town of Kymi. Leaving it behind we were soon out in the open sea. The Aegean graduated in shades of aqua to turquoise to navy as the water became ocean depth.

Hunched and alone, cold now in my white deck jeans and my short sleeved, blue and bright white sailor shirt, I crossed my arms over my chest and allowed the tears to coat my cheeks like wallpaper glue that had leaked from its lid. I just let the tears be light ones, that didn't make my eyes red or my nose stuffy. The last thing I wanted now was to be noticed.

The next hour was grueling for me, as I realized that I was drawing ever farther away from Miklos and all possibility of safety. But perhaps we were going to a more populated island and I could plead for help or try to escape when we got there. But those hopes were soon dashed. An island did rise before us, and it was small but there was enough land to have a mini ecology. There was a hill like a tiny mountain. A beach area and a lot of green trees. I could only see the side but the land curved out and in again, like the edge of a peanut. The boat curled in, headed for the edge of the island that jutted out in sharp ridges. And yet as we got closer I saw a brief dock, drilled into the rock. We swept an arc and backed in, the engine sputtering out as we drifted now to our goal. The bully of the back seat leapt out onto the dock while the boat was still moving. If I could've crowded by the driver I would've tried to slip away and escape. But I could see it was no use. The boat was tied secure, and the pair of thugs reached for me. I was a package to them, docile and weak in between their greater strength.

But as they got me on dry land I began to wake up. We stepped off the dock and a narrow path cut through some lush grass and stubby brush where the terrain took a dip and then ascended. I walked without pulling until we had cleared the narrowest part of the trail. But as soon as I saw my chance I threw myself backward, twisting my arms and falling to my backside. But the bully man stopped me from running within seconds by the kicking me as hard as he could in my shin. Pain was like a cramp and my leg buckled when I tried to stand on it.

I was scooped up under my elbows on either side and dragged again.

"Why are you doing this?" I asked in fright.

Their answer was simple, a back-smash of a man's elbow under my chin. After that I kept my mouth shut.

The narrow trail never did open up very far. We cleared a rise, and now I could see that ahead of us about a half a mile was a small set of buildings, and they were built right against a rocky backdrop of a rugged crest. We were crossing the skinny island from one side to another.

There were a few outbuildings. They were squat rectangles built in tan and white stone. But the main building was huge, tall and wide and heavy with windows and grandeur. It looked like someone who was born practical had drunk too much wine and dreamed of a powerful castle. There was a turret at one side, battlements on the other, and a widow's peak complete with lookout windows and a flag. It was vulgar somehow, unctuous, prideful, and lacking in propriety. I didn't like it at all.

We didn't go in the main doors. We went off to the left of them, and down some stairs into an outdoor stairwell and up to a locked door. The driver pulled out a shiny new key and unlocked the heavy door. I was taken inside, feeling more and more as if I'd never be heard from again. We went down a white hallway, around a corner, into gray walls and regular overhead lights, crowned in plain circular covers. Either I was in an underground hospital or a spy movie. But surely this wasn't real life. I had value to these people, and what it was I didn't know. Was it simple and animalistic? I was a girl, young and presentable, desirable in the very fact that I was unable to fight back? Was I to be some sort of slave?

Fear made my footsteps feel mushy, as if I were still at sea fighting the waves and my foot sinking fathoms each stride forward. We pushed through double doors. I viewed the intricacy of a lab, with counters, test tubes, and glass fronted cabinets. Then we pushed through a second set of double doors. Here was a room that had no furniture, except for a long table and two chairs. The bully took my arms and plunked me into one. He handcuffed my wrists to the chair seat handles. And then both of the men left.

I sat alone. The building wasn't silent—it was filled with a deep rumbling engine or furnace sound, as if there was a massive heart of generators built into the rock beneath us and these hallways were the veins. It throbbed, but provided no heat. I was shivering, missing my white windbreaker that had been tucked through the handle of my suitcase. There were goose bumps on my arms. A cold draft of wind streamed from somewhere and hit bare skin. I felt cold inside as well, quaking from my chest. In a nervous gesture I was pulling at my hands, twisting them inside the cuffs, feeling the pressure of the cold metal. I pulled the chain taut, and the skin at the base of my hand pinched upward, but the ring of the cuff wouldn't move over the place where my thumbs bulged. The wooden chair scooted as I struggled. A part of me wanted injury, insisted on bruised wrists, so that I could prove that I yearned for freedom. I felt stuffy all of a sudden, unable to breathe.

And then the double door opened and a man stood partway in it, his arm on the door while he paused with his head turned to talk to someone behind him.

"I don't have time for a meeting right now," he was protesting, his voice impatient. "I've told you that if you want me to complete the scans that you can't interrupt me about every trivial question you have."

He was answered; I could hear a murmuring reply.

"Oh, all right then! But after that let me be for a while!"

Whoever he was, he was convinced to see for himself, and he turned toward me and shoved the doors all the way open. He was pushing up some eyeglasses as he passed through. The doors banged behind him as he came to an abrupt stop.

I didn't look up at first. I was still pulling at my bonds, lifting the chair under my own weight to travel in a quarter-inch scoot across the floor. But I sent a quick glance his way, and then, another.

My perceptions took a nosedive. My breath was closed off into a dizzy swirl. Things blurred, but I could see the man's face. Reddish-brown hair, streaked with gray. A lean and rangy physique, slender in a white lab-coat. Height too, he must be six-feet-tall at least. But that didn't matter. He took off his glasses, but by then I already knew. His eyes were an unusual shade of green—herbal green, just like mine. There was no point in doubting. Transfixed, my hands locked to my side, I knew I was staring at my father for the first time in my life.

Chapter Twenty

My father stared at me, with growing dismay on his face. I saw his cheeks go red, and then watched the color recede and leave him pale. But like the others he seemed somehow connected to, he didn't start talking to me, even to reassure me. What I feared and questioned had no value, as if I were of so little importance that I wasn't worth the time it would take to talk. I saw him swallow, heavily, and then he turned and strode out. He began to shout as soon as he cleared the frame, and I could hear his words, every time the door swished back open a few inches from the heat of his agitation.

"So, I see how it is now!" he yelled. "All of your pretty words about the good of mankind? Just a lie."

And then the door completed its swaying and stilled itself, shutting off noise.

I sat and struggled with tears. It became my whole focus to keep my composure, to prevent the tears from overfilling me and spilling out everywhere. If I gave into them, I would have no control over anything.

A short time later the doors opened again. The fearsome twins pushed them open like sentinels. Someone spoke, but it wasn't my father and it wasn't the twins.

"We'll give you a few minutes alone with her, Fromme," the voice said. "But then the reunion must end so you'll get back to your work. We can't have delays, now can we?"

My father came back in the room, but he didn't look very happy about it. And yet his eyes were attached to the sight of my face.

"Was it necessary to hurt her?" he asked the twins.

The question was rhetorical, it seemed. The sentinels stepped away once he had passed through the doorway and left us alone again.

My father didn't waste any time. He dragged the other chair over and sat knee to knee with me.

"Listen," he said. "This isn't going to be easy. Those men out there, they want me to formulate something that… well, which might have different applications than the ones which I want to use it for. Dangerous applications, do you understand? That's why I was hesitant to receive their financial support. When I entered this field, I decided to dedicate my life to it. To help mankind, not to hurt it! So you must realize that I can't just …"

I had control of myself now. I was still shaking inside, but my father was addressing me, and sounding apologetic. I tried to grasp his meaning.

"Are you saying you're some sort of mad Scientist, like they film in those TV shows? And they want you to create a type of toxic poison?

A bit of humor lit his white face.

"I'm not mad."

"No, of course not. That was a stupid question. It's just this little island with no other people on it, like a fortress. And those long starchy hallways and locked doors and a mysterious laboratory underground. Father, what are you? And why have these men taken me?"

"So you know I'm your father, then?"

"Yes. June described you to me in her latest letter when she sent your address."

"How could she know my address?"

"You mean you didn't write to her, telling her you wanted to see me?"

I figured he couldn't blame me if my voice sounded unsteady.

"I didn't. I knew it would be unsafe for me to reveal that I had a child to anyone. In my field of chemistry, it's better if I don't have a weakness that could be used to sway my morals. But this is my fault. They must have found my letters."

"You mean you kept all of June's letters? But she never writes much."

"I couldn't bear to throw them out. They had your pictures, and sometimes a bit of news about you."

"Oh!"

"You're crying!"

I sniffed and controlled myself. I found that I liked the idea of him saving my mother's letters because of my pictures, and craving news about me. But I was still scared.

"Father, please let me go away from here. I don't mind meeting with you sometime if you like, but not like this."

"I'm sorry, but that's the one thing those men won't allow me to do. I've been working with some rare plant life discovered on one of the remote mountains in Northern Greece. Mixed with other chemicals, I stumbled onto a powerful poison last year. I sought to study the mixture, not to harm but because it also caused some bacteria and some green material to flourish. But research can't go on without funding, and in finding that I had to take a few risks. Now they've shown me their true intent. These men don't like my focus. They want me to go the other way in my experimentation, not to find a mixture that produces healthy crops and bacteria, but to process and intensify the plant's toxic properties. They won't let you go, I'm afraid. Not until they persuade me to do what they want."

My breath thinned and I felt pinched. I wanted to be selfish. To insist that he do whatever was needed to get me out of here. I was terrified. But a small amount of movement at the door reminded me that they hadn't given us much time. My breaths were quick and choppy as waves of anxiety, disbelief, and the intense desire to escape coursed through me. He was talking about creating a poison that these men wanted to use. I couldn't be naïve. My father was in a position of heavy responsibility, and I, because I could be pained and injured and was his child, could be used to motivate him to design that poison. I didn't feel very noble. I knew I might give into weakness later. But it was the first time I'd ever seen him. I liked his face. And there was only one gift I could give my father. I leaned forward, wishing I could release my hands and touch him or give him a hug.

"I understand," I said in a voice little louder than a whisper. "You can't formulate something bad even to save me. Don't do it, Father. No matter what, you must promise me not to let them use you to create a poison that could hurt or kill other people. Whatever's going on, I'm just one person."

He was staring at me, speechless, and for the first time I saw a fear mirrored in his eyes to the way I was shaking inside. He put a trembling hand to his face, and then he reached out and touched my cheek and sifted his fingers through my hair.

"I'm sorry, Therese," he whispered back. "But don't worry. I'm not stupid, after all. I'll figure out something. There'll be a way to get us both out of here, all right?"

The door twitched, and right on cue. The thugs had a time limit, and it made me wonder if they were fans of late-night TV like I was. There was so much time allotted to the scientist and his captive daughter, before the scientist was returned to his lab, looking miserable as he measured and mixed his chemicals to the brink of insane discovery. I wondered where the American spies were or the men from U.N.C.L.E.? Were they going to explode the island fortress just as the suave bad guy had his finger on the red button? The door pushed open and I thought I was wandering from reality a bit.

The twin sentinels came in. My father stood up and in front of me, blocking me from their view. I had to lean out to see the third man that entered. He was a sedate man, brown-haired, middle-aged, and not fat or thin. He was shorter than my father by three or four inches. He was wearing a light brown polyester sports coat, buttoned once in the middle over a black turtleneck.

"Liar," I heard my father hiss.

"Before a space can be cleared, a mess must be made," the fellow answered. "Before a government can be guided in the right direction, a threat must be experienced. Why did you suppose anyone would be interested in your soft little vitamins, and your insecticides and your fertilizers? Those in control don't want health for their populace. They want to keep them sick and old and focused on their troubles. Otherwise too many would desire the freedom at the top. There's only room for so many leaders. Don't pretend that you didn't understand that."

"And there's only so many ways in this life to make a man wealthy?" my father asked. "Don't tell me you're in any position of authority with any government. You're a salesman, trying to come up with a weapon that will tempt the wrong people into giving you a large profit. That's what you're after, isn't it?"

"A man either wants wealth or power."

"I won't do it," my father pronounced, his voice shaking a little. "Therese doesn't want me to."

"Then Therese will have to help us instead," the man replied.

"What do you mean?"

"Have you had a good look at your daughter, Fromme? Did you notice perhaps that's she's too thin, and too pale? Her lungs are mostly clear now, and yet she's not quite well, making her perfect for us to begin."

"Begin what?" my father demanded. "What are you talking about?"

"She just recovered from tuberculosis. When I had Sacno make sure of that back in Seattle, you can see why we had to bring her here. She's so ideally suited; two benefits in one! We could use her to persuade you, and test the possibilities with her disease at the same time. Her body has built fresh antibodies, but she still has the lingering after-effects of the disease in her lungs. Remember that I have Doctor Pallen and Doctor Landorf to assist me. They can begin experimenting on her right away. Much of her blood must be taken, and they must cut her open and remove ..."

"No!"

"... parts of her lungs. Then they can develop a new strain of the disease that is able to live in spite of the streptomycin's that are used to treat it. So you see. I'll get what I want in the end either way. But if I get it from you, I might not have to cut it out of her."

I leaned back in behind my father's legs. My daydreams were over. This wasn't like TV at all. There was no back music, and no actor could capture the expression that had been on the man's face and I was glad. I never wanted to see it again.

Chapter Twenty-One

The twins were practical as well as unpleasant. They shoved my father aside, unshackled me from the chair, and ignored my twisting body as I craned around to catch a last glimpse of his face. They walked me down a long hallway, stopped to push me at a drinking fountain where I gulped until they yanked me from the flow, and last they put me into a bathroom. Imagining being locked in a room without facilities, I made sure to make use of this one. I looked all around for something useful, but this bathroom was empty. Not a hook on the walls, no metal spring to hang the toilet paper roll, nothing in the drawers, and not even a hand towel to dry my hands on. As soon as the toilet flushed they opened the door and grabbed hold of me again.

The room they locked me in was also empty. No chair, no blanket, no window. A hole in the door, which was a face-sized square set at five-feet-two inches above the floor. On tiptoes I could look out, and for my trouble I was rewarded a view of the two-toned gray and white wall across the hallway. I had been prudent enough to stuff extra toilet paper in my pockets. I sat down and used some to blow my nose into.

I needed that cry. My shoulders needed to heave. It was important that I pray, and beg in whispers for God to help me get out of this. When I stopped crying and cleaned up, it felt good to let my eyes slowly lose their redness and my nose to clear. Now I felt as though I could think more clearly.

In a way things weren't as bad as they had been before. At least now I knew what was going on. Why that blond man had been chasing me. It wasn't for selling me to some slobbering monster like I had dreamed the other night in a sweat. My fears were named.

But now I felt that I shared them, at least in part, with my father. I had seen his face. I knew that he was troubled by my capture. He didn't love me as a parent did a child, how could he? But he was decent enough to regret having placed me in this situation. I wondered for a moment what he must have been feeling now. Either way a massive danger was going to be developed. If my father chose to focus on creating a poison, then at least I could be saved. But I sat and imagined how difficult it would be for him to actually plan harm to others; for his mind to be the creative force that designed the gun that would be aimed at innocent victims, and his fingers to be the ones that molded the bullets and placed them in the chamber. I grew miserable again. I was being used, not as a threat to myself, but to him. No wonder the twin thugs didn't want me to talk. I wasn't a person to them. I was a weapon and a tool.

I didn't spend a lot of time contemplating my new enemies. I couldn't understand anything about them. I sat on the floor, staring at nothing. But my isolation didn't last forever. I heard the key in the door, the murmur of voices on the other side. It pushed open, but instead of it being the thugs as I expected, it was two men in lab coats. One was a portly redheaded man, and the other was gray-haired and balding. One was carrying a rack of thin rattling tubes with rubber stoppers. A long rubber strip was draped over the top. They were earnest in conversation, and they wandered into my room, pausing to illustrate a point. They weren't speaking in English or Greek, nor French or Spanish. They were talking in Swedish or Dutch perhaps.

They came up to me, and stopped again.

"Who are you?" I asked. Nothing. I tried a phrase in Greek Miklos had taught me that I wasn't sure applied. "O opoios?" I went on and said a little more in French. "Vous êtes qui?"

The two men didn't spare me a glance, as if my voice had no sound. They talked on right over me. I sat huddled in the corner with my arms propped on my knees. I stared at my visitors, feeling invisible. And then one of the men turned to me, pulling a needle out of his pocket. He reached down and tried to pick up my arm, and when I resisted, he sighed. With a grunt he got down on one knee beside me.

Poor fellow put to so much trouble, my mind thought

sarcastically, the pains of middle age. When the second man lowered himself on the other side of me with another grunt, hemming me in, I finally realized what was going on. The one with the rack of tubes handed over the rubber strip. The other fellow took my arm with a firm grip and tapped the spot inside where the hollow of the bend occurred. They were so casual that for a moment I went along with it like an obedient victim, a speechless animal set aside for lab testing. They still weren't looking at me, and forcing myself to register my own situation, I let my eye wander to the door.

My heart started beating in thunks. A long empty hallway glistened outside, tempting in its deserted beauty. The prick of the needle in my arm and the warmth of my blood escaping into the first tube passed by my notice. I built up my courage. I had the advantage of being young, with fresh muscles. No groan was required for me to get up or down. But it was awkward nonetheless. I just had to spring, and I clutched onto the material of their lab-coated sleeves to propel me. I slithered by them, felt one man's hand scrape my skin as he grabbed me, and wrenched from his grip. Unbalanced I tripped, but I was faster than they were. Out the door I ran, pulling a tube and needle out and dropping them with the rubber strip on the floor. I went right around a corner to see Thug 1 and Thug 2 standing like sentries outside of a set of double doors. My father was in there, I thought. He must be! Seeing their eyes change into fury at my escape, and hearing the lab-coats coming behind me, I did the only thing I could think of in the time allotted. I screamed, as long and as piercing as I could.

"Father!" I screeched. "Don't give in! Father! Dad!"

The thugs were upon me and I fought like a firework spinning out of control on the ground instead of taking flight. I was loud, and spitting sparks. But throwing my head back as they picked me up by the four limbs, I was rewarded. The scientist I was after, who was named Austin Fromme and was also my father, had come to the double doors and was staring at us. I kicked mightily and a lab-coat lost hold of one foot. I quickly angled it up to kick him in the nose. Ha! I got some of his blood too! I was exultant. He wouldn't think I was invisible the next time he tried to bleed me!

Then a roar of rage from the driver-thug reminded me that I had something to accomplish. I cast a wild eye backward and got my father to meet it.

"They're doing it to me anyway!" I managed to yell. "Look at my arm. They were taking my blood. Don't believe them. Don't help them. Don't ..."

With a strangulated roar I was silenced. A fist slammed into my cheekbone, and when I choked into stillness from the shock of it, he punched me again, down the back of my head toward the floor. Just like the movies I thought. The lights went out.

I woke up not long later, when I was being put down in a hospital bed, with rails alongside my arms. I was tied to it. And then, head pounding, I watched as the lab-coats stepped up from back by the door. The thugs were done securing me.

The hospital bed cranked up until my chest was elevated above my elbows. Long rubber strip around my arm; three hands out of four holding my arm steady long enough to get the needle back in. Glass tube number one being filled.

"You're monsters," I said to the fellows. "Fat, ugly, terrible men! What use do you find in living? Who wants you around?"

My voice began rising.

"I'll spit in your eye," I yelled, and knew by the way one of them flinched that they could understand me. "Worms! Losers! Low-down vermin!"

Tube number three was done and in went tube number four. I leaned my head forward and screamed in their faces. Redheaded lab-coat yanked his chin at Thug 1.

"The subject distracts us," he said, in accented English.

"I'm not a subject. I'm a girl. And you're a wicked, stinky, stupid..."

Pincer fingers squished my face. The thug moved fast.

"Shut up," I was told.

He waved a fist at me, and my head pounded in reply. Out came tube number five and in went tube number six. I closed my eyes and gave up. I let a few tears release. By the time they had finished filling tubes, I had lost count of how many they had taken.

This was incredible, I thought to myself. Things like this didn't happen. It didn't make sense anyway. People around the world still had bouts with tuberculosis, didn't they? If it was so easy to develop a dangerous strain, and these villains were so eager to do it, then why hadn't they done it before? Why hadn't they captured some other poor victim and made use of them? No. This must be a ploy, another scare tactic to motivate my father. They were going to leave me alone now. No one was going to perform surgery like that man had threatened to remove parts of my lungs. But they could show my father me in this bed, and point scalpels at me. Seeing they were serious, he would continue his experiments under duress.

These stories were helping. Although I had no assurance that any of it was true, my mind had begun to drift enough that, for this moment when I needed it, I believed what I was telling myself. I began to feel tired, and left alone at last and weary of struggling against the bed frame, I fell asleep.

Chapter Twenty-Two

When I woke up my father was standing next to me, his arm down over the rails of the bed, so he could touch my wrist. But he had his head turned away from me to talk to someone.

"I don't see why I should believe a word out of your mouth," he was saying. "Don't think I'm fooled because you've put her in this hospital bed. I watched Paolo hurt her myself."

He was answered.

"If your daughter doesn't resist, she won't be harmed."

"But she told me that they were taking her blood. She sees that you intend to make use of her anyway, and that fact is obvious to me as well."

The fellow at the door came closer. I could see him now. He was the same soulless creature who had threatened my father before.

"They took a few harmless vials, as I've told you," the man said. "It's important that you understand her usefulness. If you want to prevent real harm to her, you should produce results for us now."

I blinked in surprise. I'd been right.

"Father, they—" I began, but his fingers flashed onto my lips.

"Shhh, Therese," he said. "I know what they did. Try not to worry about anything right now. Everything will be all right. Just rest."

His soothing voice arrested me, bringing un-experienced memories of lost piggyback rides and horsey gallops on his knee. I said nothing more.

"I want a minute alone with her to reassure her," my father demanded, turning back to the man. "Let me tell her that you'll let her go when I've finished with my formulas so that she can sleep without fear of your bullies. I can't work if I'm worrying about her."

I saw his opponent narrow his eyes. Then the man shrugged.

"I'll give you five minutes alone with her," he said.

I took a deep breath of relief. I was still a prisoner, now locked to the bed instead of in a small empty room. Yet I felt that I had moved up in the world. This room looked like a hospital room. It was bigger than the little cell had been before. There were windows along two of the walls, although they were close to the ceiling and gave me little view. There were a couple of metal tables, a chest of drawers, and a small sink against the wall. And I wasn't alone, at least for the moment. My father leaned over the bed to talk to me.

"Are you all right?" he said to me. "Paolo hit you hard."

"Yes, my head hurts but not bad. I was just dazed, I think, not really knocked out."

"Listen, Therese. I really am going to get us out of here. I have a few ideas."

"But, we can't even get out of this basement! I saw that the driver thug had the key when they brought me here from the boat!"

"Oh, I can leave the building." His voice was casual.

"You can?"

"Yes, of course. I can leave the building all I like. But there's no way for me to leave the island. There's no doubt that those two are the only ones who have the key to the boat, even if I knew how to operate it. But anyway, I have free access to the rest of this small island."

"You mean, you have a key as well?"

"There's one hanging on a hook in the lab."

"I wish I could leave! Why not give me the same freedom? Can't you untie me right now?"

I captured his attention.

"I want to untie you," he said, and his voice thickened. "But we have to be smart now. We're only going to get one chance to escape, and we can't take any risks. I'm trying to convince them that I'm ready to cooperate. That seeing you hurt in the hallway scared me enough to force my hand. That way I can have full access to my lab. In the meanwhile ..."

I interrupted. He had plans to get us out and that was good. I knew I couldn't be there with him in his lab, and I understood that he couldn't let me go. But that didn't mean that I should lie here helpless.

"Excuse me," I said, leaning forward. "I have an idea."

A small smile moved his lips.

"Let's hear it."

"Get the key off the hook. Tell the thugs you need to take a walk and view the stars, to help you think. But on the way out, leave a door open. It's really late, right? And dark outside, they must be going to sleep soon. Don't leave the door open that they would expect, but an unused one—a back door."

"To what end?"

"I just think it would be good if there was more than one escape route."

"Even if you escaped from this building, you'd be stranded outside on this island. They'd find you eventually, but by then you'd be weakened by the elements and the cold of the night and your captors would be angry with you. Your over-all situation would be worse. What's the point?"

His logic caused a frown of rebellion.

"They shouldn't have everything go so easy," I growled. "Evil people should find it difficult plowing through the muck."

"And you intend to make things go as difficult as possible for them?"

He was looking more involved with me than I'd ever seen him, as if he were intrigued by my fierceness in spite of himself. To tell the truth, I was surprised as well. I'd always been a docile child, but then again, I'd been raised by a free-spirited woman who gave me my way because she believed it was right for me to have the option of pursuing it. I was more afraid than he knew, and truth be told, that was driving me more than anything. The desire to leave this bed, break out of this fortress and hide, cold but safe and able to breathe apart from my attackers was filling my mind.

"Dad, we have to try."

He let his breath out, and I felt it, warm on my arm.

"You're quite a strong person, Therese. I'm not sure you learned that from your mother. She never pushed."

"I don't know anyone else I could've learned anything from."

"And I wasn't there to teach you, is that what you're saying? I've abandoned you?"

My mind cleared of its panic and the main focus of danger long enough to look him in the eye. I bit my lip, because I realized that

I'd like to have more of a relationship with him, and I didn't want to threaten that by saying the wrong thing.

"Yes," I said. "You abandoned me. I don't need to know why right now. But I would like to know what you intend to do about it after this. How long is it going to last before you walk away from me again?"

"I can't read the future, Therese. But I'll promise you one thing. If we both get out of Patismasia and can have normal lives, I'm willing to try to be more of a father to you."

Although most people might not think much of that promise, it satisfied me. I was used to a parent who lived her life and wasn't afraid to admit it. He wasn't promising me instant success or fairy-field birthday parties. But he was opening a door, and he was willing to let me visit. I knew that anything less than the complete truth would've disappointed me anyway. I tried to reach out a hand, and then was prevented by my bonds. My father, seeing my weakness, looked down. Then he angled his hand to fit, and took hold of mine with a warm and firm grip. He leaned down close.

"Don't worry, Therese. I'll unlock a back door out of this place, and another one into my life. And I'll find a way to get us off this island, all right?"

I smiled. I found it was fun to tease him.

"Yes, Daddy," I said.

I got the first grin I'd received from him.

All of a sudden the door pushed open. I'd forgotten that we were being allotted this time to talk. My father straightened, but his hand, still connected, gave mine a squeeze. The cold fellow with the ultimatums walked back in.

"I've had a talk with my daughter," my father said to him. "I've convinced her not to resist your men. If you'll leave her alone and allow me some space to think, I'll get to work."

"You can't waste too much time," the other man said. "I'm tired of waiting."

"I just need to walk, get some fresh air, and be alone to figure out the intricacies of the formula. But if I find that you're planning on experimenting further on my daughter, I don't see why I should help you."

"The other two scientists have enough of her blood to begin testing for now. But don't take too long on your walk, Fromme. If you're not going to give me what I want and she is, I don't see why I should put up with you."

So that was it. They reached an understanding, and I lie between them. But as my father left and he threw me a last glance, he passed something on to me in his gaze. I knew he was going to remove the key from the hook on the wall, and I knew he was going to concede to my wishes. He was going to leave a back door open. Now all I had to do was figure out a way to escape from this bed.

Chapter Twenty-Three

Despite all my grandiose thoughts and plans of escape, I had to lay back and catch my breath after a few moments. Wrestling with my bonds made my stomach churn. I remembered when one of my friends at school had hit her head. The doctors said she had a concussion. That night when I had come over to her house to visit her, I'd found her mother cleaning up a big mess where she had vomited. I swallowed and tried to relax my stomach. Perhaps I had the same thing. I'd lost consciousness, even if it was only for a moment. Those wretches tying my hands apart like this! What if I had to throw up too, all over my new bright white and blue sailor shirt? I imagined not being able to wipe my mouth afterward. Or what if I had to scratch my nose? I felt a little claustrophobic, but then I remembered the lab-coat's face when I'd kicked him in the nose. I smiled to myself and having nothing else to do but wait and no aspirin for my headache, I fell asleep.

My sleep was fitful, for the knowledge that something was wrong kept playing itself out in the back of my mind. The term 'sitting duck' meshed with the old nursery rhyme that I remembered called *The Land of Counterpane*. The bed was the sea, and its boundaries were small. I swam around like a bright target and waited to be plucked from safety. When I came from a place of troubled sleep to the realization that someone was touching me, I reacted like a frightened child. My eyes flew open and I shrank back, a screaming gasp pushed out of my lips.

"It's all right," a voice said. A voice that was rich with Greek accent, and familiar. I blinked in the dim light; for some time while I slept the overhead light had been turned off and no smaller lamp had been left on to illuminate the room I was in. The only light came from the round circular modules in the hallway, shining through the glass-fronted double doors. A curly head was leaning over me, and my arms were being tugged.

It was Miklos, and he was untying me from that dreadful bed. Instead of the nightmares I had been fending off, the answer to my daydreams had arrived. I stared at his intent profile as he worked on the wrist that was farthest from him. He was muttering a constant stream.

"You're swearing at me, Miklos!" I managed to say, but my voice was thin.

"No, Pouli. I'm not swearing at you."

"They took my ... ow," I said, as he had switched to my ankles. "They took my tenny rompers."

"Your 'tenny rompers'?"

"My mother calls them that. She means my tennis shoes. Isn't that cute?"

"Very cute," he agreed, but his voice sounded blunt.

Suddenly it all rushed in, and I stared at him rubbing my ankle where the red lines were. He had come for me! He was here inside this fortress, and soon my captors might return and discover him! And then what? What did they need him for? I sat bolt upright.

"Miklos, you have to get out of here before they find you!" I exclaimed.

"Then come on and we'll go."

"Oh, I can't leave!"

"And why not? Do you want to stay with men who tie you and bruise your face?"

"No, of course not. But I ..."

I gasped again, for I heard noises in the hall.

"Quick, Miklos! Get under the bed! If they find you here, you'll be caught too."

His eyes narrowed.

"You won't be able to help me then!"

That got his cooperation. He slipped down in one flash of movement and slid under the bed just as the door opened. I was sitting up, and rubbing my wrists. The fellow at the door, Thug Two as I called him, took one look at me and had a few things to say. It seemed to be my privilege to have men swear at me whenever they saw me.

"You untied yourself somehow, you little—"

Whatever he called me, it sounded impressive. I'd gotten under his skin, I could see. He strode across the room and pounced. I saw him lift his hand and I ducked and covered my head.

"My hands were hurting!" I protested. "I just wanted to rub them! Please don't hit me!"

My pleading voice slowed his rage. No doubt it surprised him to hear it. But I was thinking of Miklos, and how I knew that he wouldn't stay contained in his hiding place if he heard Thug Two attacking me. The fellow grabbed me and pried my hands apart.

"Now I use handcuffs," he growled. He put the words to action and the cold metal was soon clicked into place around my wrist and the other side against the metal rail. My heart sank. I hadn't even gotten the opportunity to stand on my feet before my freedom was snatched away. The fellow grabbed my jaw and squeezed hard. He leaned in till his hissing breath was an affront to my face. "Try to escape again," he said, using a minimal of words, "and I'll punish you." He threw me back against the pillows, turned his back on me, and left.

A moment later Miklos rose, and he moved slow. He stood, turned slightly, and glared at the door.

"Miklos," I said. A few seconds passed. "Miklos!"

His face returned to me, but the expression I saw was unlike anything I had ever seen from him. He was angry. Very angry.

"Miklos," I whispered.

"I'll get you free from those handcuffs," he said, pulling himself together with an effort. "There'll be something I can use."

"No, you should just get out before that thug comes back. How'd you get here? How'd you find me?"

"On my boat! Remember, I had your father's address. I was able to find this small island. Me and Andros ..."

"You brought Andros?"

"And Myron. He hadn't gone back to Crete yet."

"But where are they now?"

"They're with the boat, pulled into the other side of this island from the dock. They're waiting for us."

"And how did you get in this building?"

"I got upstairs first, but I didn't find you there. I saw a few men sleeping in grand bedrooms. So I came to search down here in this basement. It's very large and I had to search for a long time to find a way in. There was an unlocked door through a supply closet; I came in that way."

I clapped in quiet delight.

"That's because of me! I told him to leave a door unlocked!"

"You told who?"

"My father, Miklos! He's here! He's a scientist, and they want him to create something terrible! They sent that letter to my mother those weeks ago, pretending to be him. They wanted to lure me here, and when I caught the flight to Greece, they must've thought their ploy had worked. They sent that blond man to make sure I came to the right place. But I kept tagging along with you instead, and they must've been confused. So Stubbo chased me, and scared me and threatened me. Until at last, when I was close and at Kymi, they sent the other two thugs to pick me up. They told my father that they could make use of me, because I had tuberculosis. They told him they were going to develop something to hurt people, either because he created it, or by experimenting on me. Isn't that awful?"

"Yes. They should be speared, and then shot."

The casual tone of bloodthirstiness made me blink. But I shook my head.

"So you see how dangerous they are," I told him.

"I'm not leaving here without you."

"And my father!"

"All right then, we'll take your father too."

"This isn't a joyride, Miklos. The decision you make now could mean your death, or your brother's or your best friend."

"And your life, Pouli? That means nothing?"

I reached out with my free hand and tugged his shirt.

"Go to the boat and see if you can call for help," I urged. "We'll sleep here, with the villains, all unsuspecting. It's the best way."

I felt the muscles under his shirt move, tense and release. But he made his decision.

"I'll go out to the boat," he said in a low rumble. "I'll go to the boat and talk to Myron and Andros. We'll see if we can get help, and I'll find something to free you. But don't think I'll be gone for long. I'm staying nearby to you, do you understand? And nothing you say will stop me."

"But what'll you do?"

"If these villains sleep, all unsuspecting, I'll let them live till we get you out of here."

I had to laugh. At that moment I agreed with him that alone he was able to accomplish anything, even taking down a soulless man, a couple of lab-coated, middle-aged scientists, Thug One and Thug Two, and possibly Stubbo by now just to round out the party. Our heads were close as I sat up and he stood next to me, and the kiss was natural, the two of us coming together at the same moment. I held his shirt, and his hand wrapped around my cheek. The dim lights hid us, and danger hovered at the door, but we took the moment and owned it.

"Therese," he whispered, and I heard longing in his voice.

"Please be careful when you sneak out," I replied.

"I don't want to leave you here."

"Just go and do what you have to do. I'll wait right here for you to come back."

We both looked down at the handcuffs, ensuring that I could do nothing else. And then, with reluctance, he pulled away.

"I'll come back as soon as I can," he said. "Don't worry. I'll get you out of here. You'll see!"

A moment later I watched, as his head was a silhouette against the door. Seeing no one outside he pushed it open with caution, and then he was gone. I sat tense for the next twenty minutes until I allowed my heart to start beating in a normal rhythm. No alarms were sounding. He must've gotten out of the building. With relief I laid back against my pillows. There was no way I could sleep. Outside it was midnight, or beyond, but in this building my father was working in his lab and I was unable to accomplish anything. I was a motivating factor to two men determined to help me, but I wanted to help them instead. They had both promised to do something, and I hoped that whatever their plans were that they would work together somehow to free all of us. Morning seemed a long while away.

Chapter Twenty-Four

The next hour passed slowly. I'd had a couple of naps in the past several hours, and had been visited by Miklos, so I was wide-awake. In my short life, I hadn't experienced many situations that confounded me like this one. My mother had been a marvel, and I was just now realizing the full extent of her ability. Somehow, she had kept me on a careful leash, while at the same time making me believe that I was the one telling her what I wanted to do and where I wanted to go. Desiring a place of safety, I came home every night, and cleaned my room, and had a bedtime (although often I sat in bed and watched the late movie). And she, by making sure our little house was always there to fall back on, came home too. Together we went about our business, laughed about the people who moved in and out of our lives, and even, once I was big enough, shared clothes and did each other's hair. Now I lay in bed and missed her. I missed my safe bedroom, eating cinnamon toast at one in the morning while TV spies crept down the starched hallways of their enemy fortresses.

If only real-life thugs could be as stupid as those on TV. And if only I had the certainty that Miklos and my father were going to get out of this alive. I no longer thought of myself, for I was becoming used to being helpless, and a pawn. I'd been a prisoner for just a few hours, but it was enough to change my life.

Somewhere nearby, my father worked in a lab, but he seemed a thousand miles away. Somewhere outside, within a mile or so of me, Miklos walked or hid, but he needed to wait until help arrived before he could do anything. All of a sudden restlessness took hold. My will had been sleeping, while I reacted to the shock of my situation. But now I wanted to charge from the room and change things. I wanted to go and find my father and show him Miklos and … but I held in a sigh. I shouldn't do something stupid that could bring harm to either man no matter how I was tempted.

A shadow moved at the door, and I looked up, expectant. But it was just Thug 1, checking to see that I was still at my post. I looked away and he left. And then I frowned. I decided that the two were going to check up on me periodically all night, but I probably had at least a half an hour before the next sighting.

I got up on my knees. One hand was chained to the railing, but the handcuff gave me some leeway. With some maneuvering I got out of the bed, and stood on my feet with the railing as my escort. I looked down under the mattress and heavy metal frame, stood back up again, and grinned. The old hospital bed was on wheels. The handcuff slid along the railing until I was near the head of the bed. It was weighty, and it squeaked. But it moved.

"Come on, Bedhead," I murmured to it. "Let's take a walk."

It was easy to reach the door once the bed got going on the smooth linoleum floor. The hallway outside was empty and the door was unlocked. My furniture companion and I pushed the double doors open, where they bumped into the metal frame, and then slipped out into the freedom of the hallway. Steering in a straight line was difficult, and I had to adjust my aim often. The hallway had three normal doors with the small square in them, and down at the end where it turned a corner, there was another set of double doors. I huffed and waded up to them. Standing sideways next to the bed, I got a look into the frosted glass.

There was a lab on the other side, but it wasn't the one I first saw when I entered the facility, and it didn't contain my father. But I could see a lot of equipment all around, cluttering up several tables and counters, a blackboard with a lot of scrawled hieroglyphics, and at last something that I recognized.

The little tray of glass tubes with their rubber stoppers was visible, filled with my blood. Thieves! Combined they had taken at least a pint of my blood, or perhaps more. I did feel weak, but who knew if that was due to their vampirism, or to the loving touch of Thug Two, or because I was still scared like a rabbit. I wanted to push into the lab and destroy all the vials. But Bedhead might take down more of the lab than planned. No. I pushed on.

It was fun to waddle around the corner, and the bed and I

crashed into a wall. I held in a giggle and listened, terrified at the same moment. No one came, so I continued my journey. Again this hallway had three normal doors with little square windows, and two sets of double doors. I could see that the closer set of doors belonged to a room that wasn't darkened. The lights in that lab were on.

Now I paused, heart pounding. Were my thug guards in there? Or their stony boss? But it was all crazy anyway. I was doomed to be caught, and then no doubt they would handcuff all my limbs to the inside of a closet. I didn't care. I had this moment of freedom now; even if the outside door was locked and there was no way I could lift Bedhead up the cement stairs if I did manage to break outside. I pushed and slipped barefoot down the hall, angled in the general direction, built up some speed, and crashed right into and through the set of lighted double doors. I had come calling on whoever populated that lab.

But it was all right. My noise and surprise entry caused a reaction, but it was my father who wrenched around and dropped a beaker that shattered with a tinkling crash. His eyes blinked wide at my arrival and his glasses slipped down his nose.

"Therese!"

My tone went cheerful.

"Hi Daddy!" I said, right before I burst into tears.

His eyes blinked even wider, but his mind moved fast. He crunched over broken glass and reached my side in seconds. He took the railing and folded it down with one efficient movement. He put his hands on my waist and picked me up to sit on the bed, and then he pulled it the rest of the way into the lab so the doors could swing shut. Then, once I was propelled near the wall and not in plain sight of the double doors he plunked his hands on his hips and glared at me.

"Are you trying to get yourself attacked again?" he demanded. "Didn't I tell you I was working on a way to get you out? What sense is it for you to escape to me here?"

My chin wavered.

"You mean you didn't want to see me?"

"Therese, have they doped you or something? Stop acting like a child!"

"As if you would know what a child acts like."

"I've told you there's no point in you trying to escape. You'll just make them angry, and they'll hurt you again."

"But Dad, I have something important to tell you! He came! Miklos came here to find me!"

"What are you talking about?"

"Miklos!" I insisted, for I couldn't imagine that he wouldn't know of someone so important for a moment. "My friend here in Greece. He was with me when they took me! He had stepped away for a moment to use the phone, and when he came back I was gone, so he followed me here, and Dad! He came in a boat!"

"Are you all right, Therese? Did they hurt your head more than I realized? Blast! You need a hospital!"

Time was being wasted, and I knew we didn't have much. I grabbed his lapel with my one free hand. I yanked his face close.

"Dad. I'm fine. Miklos came. He snuck into my room because you unlocked the door. He couldn't free me from this handcuff. So he snuck back out to see if his friend and his brother could get us help. I'm not crazy, and I'm not delirious. I'm telling the truth."

Several long seconds ticked by while he considered my words.

"You're telling me," he spelled out at last, "that you've got some fellow, roaming around after you on this island?"

"Yes!"

"Why? Is he your boyfriend?"

"What difference does that make?"

"Because I want to know why some fellow is so determined to hang all over my daughter!"

"For heaven's sake!" I hissed, incredulous. I was having my first argument with my father, and he was treating me like I was a teenager. I decided to distract him by giving out a few orders. "Get me out of these handcuffs! Take me out of this building, now before Thug One or Two spots us, all right?"

"So we can find your boyfriend?"

I stared at him. This was the strangest thing that had happened yet. But I put in some verbal effort.

"He's my best friend, Daddy! He saved my life when I was ten and June had brought me here to Greece on a vacation. I've been writing him all these years. He's stood by me through all of this too. He came here now not because he's determined to get me into bed, but because he's a good man and he cares. You understand?"

"And you say this Miklos has a boat."

"Yes, now can you get some tool to free me with? We don't have much time!"

"But you say he went to his boat to talk to his friends. I don't suppose you know where on this island their boat is. So in essence, there's nothing we can do but wait for him to return."

"Well, we don't have to stay here in this lab, do we Daddy? Let's go outside away from these people while we wait for him. Please? You don't want to leave me down that long hallway alone, do you? Those thugs come in and hurt me!"

I poured on a few tears. They were easy to produce and he would've had to be made of stone to resist them. I told myself that it was for his own good, but in reality I was afraid of the thugs and saw no reason to wait for more of their company. The tears grew thick. The sight of them rolling down my cheeks defeated his doubts in seconds.

"All right, Therese, don't cry!" he begged. "If you want to wander all night in the dark and make the thugs as you call them mad, we'll do it, even if this Miklos is a figment of your imagination!"

I sniffed. I dried my face with the back of my hand while he leaped over to the other side of the room and rummaged in a drawer. He came back with the last tool I expected, holding it up with a grin. Giant bolt cutters.

Chapter Twenty-Five

"We use these to cut open chains wrapped around the delivery crates," my father explained to me as he arranged the cuffs so he could free me from them. "The crates are chained for security purposes, because they hold acids and other dangerous chemicals. I'm putting your handcuff chain on the bed rail now. Turn your face away, Therese. The broken chain might fly off a segment when I cut it."

When we had freed me from the cuffs, all except for a manacle bracelet left on my wrist, and snuck down the hallway, we avoided the thugs with ease. My father knew where they went and he was familiar with all the rooms in the facility. Soon we went into the storage closet, where indeed there was an outside door.

It felt so good to slip out into the night. The tiny edge of the moon curled and the stars pierced bright on this small island. It was strange to be in a place that had no roads, no telephone wires, no sidewalks or stores or cars. Here there was just the landscape, tilting up toward the island's only hill to our right, the sound of waves crashing against the rocky edge of the island up ahead, and the lower land of scrub and blanketed gray silhouettes to the left. The velvety air, cooler than my skin, took away some of my weariness.

And yet I still clung to my father's arm. My head ached, and I took a deep breath and relaxed my shoulders and my jaw, which I had been clenching in nervousness until we could get out.

"Toward the water behind the buildings there'll be rocks and knotted trees and more places to hide," my father said.

"Yes, all right."

We scurried away from the facility and the lights. The ground in front of us cushioned our steps, but there was rock here too, which I noticed when I stubbed my bare toe on a hillock. I hopped for a moment, my father glanced down at my white feet distracted, and then we hurried on.

Yet after a moment we both sensed someone behind us. I could tell by the way my father threw his head back over his shoulder for a look at the same moment I did. It was hard not to make a comment. I let him lead and kept my head to the rear, and yet all I saw was the wiggle of a bush. Up ahead the hill came down to meet us, bowing upward and owning the surface of the land till you either had to climb or move to the left to free yourself from the wall. It was there we both stopped and turned.

"Who is it?" I asked.

"I can't tell."

"If it's one of the thugs, why don't they come out? Or are there other scientists on this island that I don't know about?"

"Not right now. I believe you've met the whole group."

We weren't whispering, but our voices were so quiet I needed to place my head right next to his to hear. And then I gasped and clutched harder at my father. A thick shadow separated from the path above us and floated down, then stepped out to where the opening in the sky made it clear to see.

"Miklos!" I exulted, though I managed to keep my voice down. And yet my father stepped forward and shielded me. The three of us came together and met, in the small clearing at the base of the hill.

"Who are you?" my father demanded. I moved to speak, but his hand held me firm.

"I'm Miklos," my friend said. "I came to help."

"Help yourself to my daughter, you mean? Traveling around with her in a country she doesn't understand, while she gives you her friendship and her ..."

"Dad!" I protested. "Now isn't the time! And what are you saying anyway? I told you about Miklos!"

But Miklos had kept silent, not straining forward to meet my father's challenge. An awkward silence fell, but soon we were all looking behind us, wondering how long until someone dangerous came to join the party. At last it was Miklos who spoke, helping us all to move beyond the moment.

"You fear for your daughter," he said, "and I'm a stranger to you. For now you'll have to trust her, if you can't trust me. There's a boat, waiting there down at the foot of those rocks. Come and I'll show you."

My father, holding on to me now, was shaking. I knew it wasn't from fear or anxiety. He was charged, and ready to defend. It must be difficult, I thought, to be thrown into parenting without warning. All of a sudden he had a full-grown daughter taken prisoner in front of him, requiring that he watch while I got hurt. I had convinced him to leave his comfortable lab and run out into the night to hide with me. And now here was this young man, putting himself forward into my life. And here was I, talking about Miklos with starry eyes.

"He's not the enemy," I said into his ear. "He's my friend. Come on, Father. It'll be all right."

"Go on then," he said, but he was still talking to Miklos. "Take us to this boat of yours."

Miklos broke out into his joyous grin.

"Yes, I'll take you! She's a fine boat!"

He went a little fast, and my father was determined to stay between us, it seemed. So, that left me in last place, with the shrubs underfoot giving way to sand and silt and rock dust. Miklos stopped and pointed upward.

"This way," he said. "Is better."

Up on the rugged hillside I could see what he meant, for the hump of land leveled out after a few feet's sharp climb above my head and gentled to the water edge a few hundred feet farther on. It was too bad we never made it all the way there. Miklos went halfway up and perched, leaning his warm veined hand down to us. My father didn't grasp it for long, and made his own way. I was more willing to take hold.

Just as I reached up there was a blast of sound from behind us, and a chip of hillside broke off and blew away next to my hand. It took me a few seconds to figure it out, but Miklos was already moving.

"Therese!" he hissed.

From behind me I heard a rush of movement. Pounding footsteps. Another crack of noise, only this bullet barely missed me as I ducked and slipped back to level ground. Miklos jumped, off the hillside where he had been attached, landed next to me, and yanked me with him off to the side to curl in behind the rock wall. Then he pushed by me and leaped away into the darkness.

The thugs had arrived, one within shooting distance, and the other more distant. I peeked and saw it all, the white square face of the thug as he slowed to take aim at me, my father backing off the hillside with his arm outstretched, and Miklos. He was running back toward the thug with the gun. The fellow saw his movement, and readjusted his aim. I heard the gun go off when Miklos tackled into him. That brought me out of hiding. My arms were reaching, and my father was protesting. But soon I was upon the double-knot of Miklos and the bad man. The gun was lifted high, with two hands fighting for it, one pale and blocky and the other lean and brown.

I did what any healthy young woman would. I went right for his hair. Thug Two had short hair like his partner, but there was enough for me to yank into. I waved his head back and forth and hung off him like a leech or a clinging banshee. The other thug and my father soon arrived to join in, and there we were, like a dancing clump of piranha fish tearing over gun meat. The gun went off again, shooting a bullet into the sky. I was about to wonder where bullets like that ended up, when the bar of arms that we were all aimed at bent and angled sideways.

Voices spoke, all male, offering threats. But one made sense. It was the newcomer thug. He stepped out of the throng and grabbed onto me.

"I have a gun too!" he bellowed. "I'll shoot her!"

I felt a cold muzzle against my forehead.

That did it. Two against one, yet Miklos and my father let their hands drop away from the fellow they had been fighting.

It had all been for nothing. The idiots had taken control again. Soon they would put us back into that fortress; only this time there would be no freedom to take hospital beds on journeys or for my father to wander under the stars. I looked at Thug Two and despised him. The man sized up the situation. His partner, older and more superior, had arrived to take control. The girl who caused so much trouble was in hand, again. The scientist, who had never been much of a problem before, was standing quiet and worried for his child. But there was one other that he could deal with. I saw the knowledge enter the man's eyes. What did he need Miklos for? Nothing but the sport of taking his excess thuggery out on somebody. The man grinned. He turned to focus on Miklos.

I realized he was going to kill him! And who would ever know if he did, out here on this deserted piece of rock? But he had that gun and no one to stop him from shooting him!

A point of insanity exploded right out of the center of my brain. I was a shriek, a bursting animal that clawed and leaped. No! Not Miklos. That was the only thought that drove me.

I dove to the side, screaming, and the thug threatening me had to wrestle with me. I tripped and tangled our legs as I plowed forward. Miklos watched, his eyes large, but what really surprised me was my father. He took advantage of the distraction and pushed Miklos' thug, hard, and the gun went off for the fifth time.

My father must've come to the same conclusion I had. He may not have been sure if he wanted Miklos interested in his daughter, but the three of us had become an instant team, banded against a shared threat. I was still out of control, in front of the other thug now, trying to shield them from his arm and his gun. My father was moving beside me, digging in his pocket, pulling out a tube that he broke into a handkerchief. He charged forward and bent over Miklos's thug's back, until the cloth was on the man's face. Miklos was helping and within seconds Thug Two had slipped to his knees with a groan. The man passed out, overcome by a chemist.

My two men turned, and Thug One saw that he was alone now. He was facing a hysterical girl, a determined Scientist with some sort of drug-soaked rag, and a stranger. He stared at the three of us. He lifted his gun and stopped to glare at me. I was the one who had refused to be easy bait, and I was the one he was most determined to shoot if he had to come down anyway. He spoke, and spelled out a few sentences to us in a language I couldn't understand. Then he aimed his gun right at my chest. His hand flexed, and his finger bore down.

And then Miklos, who was not hysterical like I had been when faced with the same sight, but controlled, dived with a roar right onto his arm. When the gun went off it sounded muffled.

My hands flew to my cheeks. The two men were on the ground, but Miklos stayed there. The awful thug got up. Now I was incapacitated. All I could understand was that Miklos lay unmoving, his head against the rock ledge.

But TV movies described scenes that had to play out right in the end, didn't they? People build relationships, and those threads tie together. When gunshots are heard, several hundred feet away from a boat that is waiting to rescue, those men on board come running. My white face lifted when I saw the two helpers dropping down from the ledge above us. It was Andros and Myron, arriving to see if Miklos needed help. My father, not as frozen as I was, bent and picked up the sleeping thug's gun. He waved it around, but I told him that Myron and Andros were Miklos' brother and his best friend. We turned.

Finally Thug One, the driver and coordinator of trauma, saw that he was outnumbered. He tossed his gun in the grass and held up his hands. My father walked right up to him and smashed his drug-soaked rag into his face and then shoved him when he toppled unconscious. Then we all turned to Miklos.

Chapter Twenty-Six

"Hurry!" my father said. "Those two will only be out for a few moments, and those up the hill may soon come running to the shots."

But despite his words my father had been the first one at Miklos' side. He had pulled him away from the rock and viewed his head before he spoke.

"Daddy!" I protested. "Miklos!"

"He isn't shot, Therese," he told me; his voice clear and firm. "He has a bump and a scrape here. He must've hit his head. In fact, I see the hole where the bullet stuck the rock above him."

Myron spoke in Greek, and my father, to my surprise, answered him with a calm and fluent reply in the same language. It annoyed me.

"Daddy, Miklos is hurt!" I demanded.

"Then let's get him out of here, all right, Sweetheart?"

"Don't 'Sweetheart' me! What if he's bad off?"

"I don't see a lot of swelling. I'm sorry but that's all I can give you. Pull yourself together, for his sake."

It was hard, but I managed to keep quiet while the three men murmured to each other and picked up Miklos with gentle care. He moaned and moved his head and my heart banged, trying to leap out of my chest and see for itself.

Myron went to the top of the ledge. Andros and my father laid Miklos up against the wall, and Andros climbed halfway. And then the three of them hauled him up in one smooth movement. None of them asked for any help from me.

As it was I felt useless anyway. My head felt thin and like it was spinning above a hot burner, touching down every now and then to make painful contact. I'd never been so frightened or so strung out on anxiety in my life.

I climbed up the rock barefoot, and I was clumsy. My foot slipped and I tore a hole in the knee of my white deck jeans. I scrambled onto the level and they stood up to proceed with Miklos when I rose unsteady behind them. And then we were hurrying, off into the night, and me tripping and dropping to the ground more than once. From behind, I heard sounds of commotion. My heart grew erratic in my chest again when I discerned what the noises were. I swung around, but my father came up to me.

"Come on, dear, not much farther," he urged. I tried to go fast, but a strange exhaustion took over my legs. "Look," my father added. "Your friend is on his feet. He's waiting for you to catch up!"

I blinked and saw it was true. Miklos, his arms draped around the two men's shoulders for support, was on his feet now and doing his best to stumble forward. My father wrapped his arm behind me and we did the same.

The trip off the rocky edge into the boat was tricky, but none of us slowed. Distant shadows were appearing on the level now. They were coming after us.

"Careful Miklos," Myron was muttering, and then he said, "I've got her, sir," a moment later. As his hands assisted me on the boat I felt a strange thing happen. I looked at him and saw 'brother-in-law' written on his face. I shook my head. I was dizzy and floundered to the side, but he supported me.

"Is all right," he said in a thick accent. "Now we take you and my brother to the hospital, and Andros calls the police."

I blinked and he looked like Myron again, a handsome Greek man of twenty-seven with a wife and two children and a younger brother who had woke up enough to say something.

"Therese, come sit by me!"

I obliged, settling down on a padded bench, so he could lean his curly head against my bright white and blue sailor shirt and get spots of blood on it.

"Red, white and blue!" I trilled, and he looked up at me.

"Are you all right, Pouli?" he asked.

I wish I could say that we made it to the hospital without incident. But the bad guys' boat was after us within fifteen minutes. It had heavy lights that pierced the night. It also had a more powerful motor. Even so, we had enough of a head start that it took till we had sighted the land around Kymi for it to catch up to us.

During that hour Miklos had bent over the side of the boat, lost his stomach, and then gone to stand next to Andros at the boat's controls. I would've gone too, but the cabin was crowded with four men, standing as men do. That left me to stumble to the back of the boat and watch for our enemies.

I could see a few of them silhouetted through the window on their power launch, but I couldn't make out their faces.

"You should've taken the keys to the boat out of his pocket when you took the man's gun," I muttered, but more to myself than because my father could hear me. I supposed that they might have had an extra pair of boat keys stashed in the fortress anyway. I had moved beyond fear now, since I was in a place of waiting, and having nothing that I could do to help the boat go faster. I was numb, and watched with a stoic expression as the other boat inched from the distance behind us to move closer.

I wondered what it was our pursuers intended to do when they caught up to us. Ram us? Open a slot window in the side of their launch, and produce a cannon? The coast of Kymi was just a half mile away now; the wide and spread out harbor and its low dark green hills all around the shoreline. When the boat behind us came close enough that I could see their faces, I wasn't surprised. Three men stood in the launch's cabin. I made eye contact with the cold leader first, and then stared at Thug Two, whose face was concentrated and a little wild, and then finally my eyes moved to Thug One. The man who had spoke to me in the dark and then pointed his gun at me; the man who was the one who made me angrier than any of them because of his control and his efficiency. The expression on that man's face woke me from my stupor. I meant to look away, to scuttle to my friends and get away from him. But the intensity in his eyes held me. He blamed me for the inconvenience of this chase. I was at fault for putting their smooth and calculated plans at risk. And I was the one that he intended to make pay for it, no matter what his boss had to say.

The knowledge of his vengeance was clear to me, so that when he stepped out of his cabin and faced me in the night wind, I wasn't surprised to see the flash of metal in his hand, reflected off of the headlamp that adorned the top of their boat.

Our launches were plowing with speed, bumping uneven with the rugged waves of the Aegean. Theirs began to pull to the side to pass us, and he lifted his gun. I backed up, but he didn't hesitate this time. He shot, and I reacted, and just then Andros veered our boat sideways to avoid theirs. It happened just like it had when I was ten years old. I flew off the end of the speedboat and landed in the cold water. And just like before, no one noticed, except for the pirate who shot at me. The bullet missed its mark, but he couldn't know that.

So there I was, bobbing in the water. Miklos had asked me if I had improved, and in truth I did swim better than I had at ten. I'd taken a few lessons the next year, and done fine until the lessons had moved to the deep end of the pool. Then I had balked, and my mother, never one to bother, had let it go. I hadn't told Miklos that I was afraid of deep water and had been since that day.

But the fear was cured now, for I was more concerned about the two boats speeding away from me and the pirates with the guns. The water, now I had gotten used to the temperature was a silky awareness up to my neck. I could see the edges of the boats getting more distant. I saw them crash together and cling. I saw them slow down. And then I thought I could make out something strange, the waves and bottoms of other boats, coming up to meet them. I blinked and strained my eyes, and barely noticed the first backwashing wave that hit and rocked my body sideways and then level again.

Now I had to paddle more, stabilize myself and concentrate on my own situation. The sound of the motors dimmed. I thought I could hear distant shouts. I paddled and grew tired and kept my head above water.

My body began to complain at me. *I was knocked senseless just a few hours ago*, it reminded me. *I've had my blood taken, and I've been terrified, and now this. I can't really be expected to maintain this vigil when I can barely swim. And there's no way I can make it to shore.*

Shhh, I told myself. *Miklos and my father might be in trouble.*

This argument continued as waves kept on striking me, dousing my cheeks and dunking my head. I paddled and floated and grew slow in the water. I coughed and floundered and sank for a moment, below the silky depths. I felt sleepy, and slowed more, and then realized I had drifted under, and curled sideways.

Perhaps again I wasn't going to make it. Perhaps the pirates had succeeded in being evil and none of us had made it. I stopped paddling for a moment to rest, bobbed and sank a few feet. I closed my eyes and righted myself, pretending to be a cork but too tired to dog paddle any more. I thought a bright flash moved over my head, but when I opened my eyes I just saw golden water.

And then I felt another presence splash into the water beside me, and strong arms encircled me and brought me to the surface.

"Hold on, Pouli," a voice said, and I smiled and let dizziness take hold.

"Dear Miklos," I murmured in return.

Chapter Twenty-Seven

"She didn't exercise prudence," my father said to the police, followed by a more exacting translation from Miklos.

"And what does that mean?" the policeman asked.

This interview was taking place at the Kymi General Hospital, where Miklos and I sat in the same room on two rolling gurneys. We were both wrapped in blankets and had both had our heads examined. The police had shown up soon after we had made it to shore, but they had been busy with their arrests and allowing the victims to be taken to the hospital. My father had already explained about the poison he had been coerced to make, and the rest of the cold man's plans. The policeman had already been kind enough to take up my wrist and unlock me from my manacle bracelet, all that was left of the handcuffs. Throughout the interview Miklos had sat quiet and supplied whatever words either my father or the policeman needed to understand each other.

I was eager to hear the interview done by my father, and glad for once that Greek men tended to turn to other men for explanations. For I was still confused as to what had happened near the end myself.

"It means that she wasn't a docile prisoner," my father explained. Miklos told the policeman what the word 'docile' meant, or so I assumed.

"Go on," the man prompted.

"They locked her up, and she got away from them. They handcuffed her to the bed and she dragged it down the hallway. She found me and made me free her and take her out into the night."

"She made you?"

"She cried and called me Daddy until I gave in."

The policeman smiled in understanding.

"Ah," he said.

"Once we got outside we found this young man, whom she had enchanted enough to come find her," my father continued.

"'Enchant'?"

"Goitevo," said Miklos.

The policeman grinned again.

"We went to escape the island, but Paolo and Dulc came running. They shot at us."

"And these two men are?" the policeman prompted.

"Thug One and Thug Two," I supplied, figuring that Miklos shouldn't be the only one who got to translate.

The policeman looked at me, and his eyes roamed up and down. I wasn't showing much to appeal wrapped in a blanket and my red hair drying in loops and whorls. But I gave out my most attractive smile. He returned to my father.

"So these two uh ... thugs shot at you, and yet you got away? How is that?"

"She made us fight them. That's how her young friend got hurt."

"But they were going to shoot Miklos," I protested. "I couldn't just stand there and let them do that!"

"And Miklos nearly got shot anyway having to protect you a moment later," he replied.

I grumbled and receded.

"His friends, who were waiting in his boat to help us escape, heard the shots and came to see. We overpowered the two men and managed to make it to his boat, but they followed us and chased us here to Kymi."

"And fifteen of our citizens took out their fishing boats and their rowboats and their other sea craft and met you?"

"Yes," agreed my father. I sat up straight in surprise. I had no idea.

"They did?" I asked. "But who were they?"

"Friends," said Miklos, with simplicity. "Matthaios and some of the others you met, Therese. Andros had called for help."

"Once the men saw they were outnumbered they put down their guns and tried to speed away," finished my father, "but they had been boarded by the friends who had come to help. They were held until you came."

"Our police have gone to their island," the policeman said. "There they found two other men, both scientists who claim to know nothing of any coercion against anyone. They say they were held prisoners as well."

"Blood suckers," I muttered.

Policeman asked for clarification, Miklos told him. They turned to look at me, and I felt shy all of a sudden.

This bold and reckless young woman they had been describing wasn't me. Was it?

The policeman sighed.

"Well, I think that's enough for now," he said, standing up and folding closed his tatty notebook. But then he turned and said something to Miklos, in Greek, which made Miklos laugh and look down. My father didn't look pleased at the joke.

"What did he say?" I demanded of Miklos as soon as he left.

"He said you light fires in men," he answered with a squint for the translation.

"What!"

"You make men do things; react strongly," my father expanded, but I got the impression that he was giving the words a much tamer interpretation. Miklos leaned back on his arms and looked up at him with his brown eyes.

"Goitevo," he said.

My heart began to thump, but my father stood up with a sigh. He held out his hand.

"You saved Therese's life, and mine too, in all probability," he said, sharing a firm handshake with Miklos.

"Thank you, sir."

"But trifle with my daughter, and I'll beat you."

Miklos stared with big eyes.

"Do you need me to translate the word, 'trifle'?"

"No, sir."

One more handshake, and the men were done talking to each other. My father turned to me.

"Therese, do you have a place to stay? Because if not, I can get you a room at my hotel here in town. I've kept one engaged for when I visited."

"Thank you, Daddy, that would be nice."

"Your friend will bring you to the hotel soon, right?"

He told us the where the hotel was located and what it was called.

"His name is Miklos, Dad."

"I know what his name is. Make sure you get plenty of rest, young man. A concussion is nothing to fool with."

"I will, sir. Just as soon as I bring your daughter to your hotel."

A moment later Miklos and I were alone at last, and free from danger. It seemed unreal.

"Are you all right?" we asked at the same moment. He smiled.

"I look better than you, Pouli."

"Oh, thanks a lot!"

"I mean, my face isn't covered in bruises."

"Covered in them?"

I scrambled to my feet and went to visit the tiny mirror that hung above the hospital sink. It was true. One eye was tinged with black, which then fanned out from my eyebrow to the edge of my hairline. Then color flowed from my cheekbone and all on one side. Even under my chin was a bruise that meandered up and swelled a portion of my lower lip. It was all there recorded, my recent experiences, marked for the world to see. And I had smiled like a fool at the policeman, thinking I was proving how attractive I was! Miklos came and stood behind me.

"You see, Therese," he said, "you look even more appealing bruised, like a child one wants to protect."

I met his eyes in the glass.

"I'm not a child," I reminded him.

He turned me around and his arms encircled me. My nose nestled under his collarbone.

"I'm just glad you're here," he breathed. I snuggled closer.

"And I'm glad you're here, too!"

"You've scared me so much, since we got back from the ferry!" he went on. "First when I discovered that you were missing, and then when I saw you so still and bruised and tied to that hospital bed."

"I was really grateful when you untied me from that bed. Thank you, Miklos."

"And when I saw that man point his gun at you ..."

"That other thug was going to shoot you first, and that scared me!"

He chuckled.

"You looked like a wild bird, then. A skinny bird with flying feathers."

"No fair!"

"'No fair'? What does that mean?"

"You understand the word 'trifle', but you don't understand what 'no fair' means?"

"I understood what the word meant by the look on your father's face."

Now I laughed at him. He pulled me close again and went on with what he was saying.

"But I was the most scared after we'd confronted those men and I realized you weren't on my boat. I'd heard a gun shot, but I didn't understand what it might've meant until that moment. We came back to find you, but I couldn't see you in the water."

"I couldn't see you, either."

"No, Pouli. You were drowning. I had to shake you awake and your lips were blue. You never did learn how to swim any better, did you?"

"Stop scolding me. Seattle isn't the best place for sunny beaches, you know."

"I heard that there are beautiful lakes and rivers all around Washington State."

"Well, okay. I guess there are. But I was afraid of the deep water after my accident. And you weren't there to teach me."

"I don't believe you're afraid of anything after tonight."

"It was fear that was making me do all the things I did."

"You're a very special girl, Therese. But back to you learning to swim. If you need me to teach you that's what I'll do, first thing, or else the third time I jump in to save you it might be too late."

"Is there going to be a third time?"

He pulled me back to stare at me, but he seemed to stop himself from saying anything more. He stroked my cheek with his thumb instead.

"You're here now. And you're exhausted, and bruised, and still damp. Besides my brother is waiting outside. He intends to drive you to your hotel and then take me to our friend's house to sleep. He says he must baby-sit me."

"Ha ha. 'Big brother is watching over you.'"

He grinned.

"From the book you read in high school, *1984*, eh, Pouli?"

My emotions took a nosedive. All of a sudden I remembered the blond block man of a few days ago. He took my letters from Miklos. He probably threw them away.

"Anyway," Miklos went on with a sigh. "I'll have to teach you to swim tomorrow."

He stood up straight and let go of me and I felt the loss. Just as we set down our blankets on the gurneys and prepared to leave the hospital in my bare feet he held out his hand and we clasped our fingers. We went outside and Myron leaped out of a jeep he had borrowed from his friend and opened the door for us.

"Now you two will go and get some rest," he said.

Chapter Twenty- Eight

When I arrived in my hotel room that my father had reserved for me, I fell into the small bed exhausted. Dawn had arrived, and the hotel staff was busy with early morning preparations for breakfast. I didn't want any. The sky was dark blue dimming into lavender and pink. I shut the curtains against the sunrise, pulled off my white deck jeans and my bra, and slept in my shirt and panties.

When I woke up it was dark in the room, and someone was knocking on the door.

"Therese!" a voice called.

I stretched and got up, stumbling in the dark to the door. I opened it and then remembered what I wasn't wearing. I hid behind it, peeking my head out. My father was standing there and I eyed him. It was the first time I'd seen him without a lab coat.

The brown and orange-checkered shirt he was wearing brought out his eyes and the salty red thickness of his hair. My eyes grew wide. He was still a good-looking man.

"Hi, Daddy," I said, rubbing my eyes with the back of my fingers.

"You've been asleep for fourteen hours," the man complained. "It's after seven in the evening."

"How do you know when I went to sleep?"

"I waited up for you and saw you come in. Alone."

I smiled.

"You're going to have to get used to Miklos, Daddy."

He must've seen the intent in my eyes.

"So you're interested in him, then?"

"Any objections?"

"I haven't been able to spend any time with you myself yet."

I froze after he said the words, as we both realized whose fault that was.

"Therese, I ..."

I held up a hand to interrupt.

"Not yet, Dad. Let's have this talk after I get dressed and cleaned up."

"All right," he agreed. "I claim dinner tonight. Miklos will have to wait. He brought your cases by the way. I'll get them for you."

"That was nice of him to take the time when he must've been tired!"

"You've been asleep all day. The police brought your purse too. They found it on Paolo's boat."

"Everyone is so kind!"

"Humph. You put a spell on that policeman just like everyone else."

"Strange words. Have I put a spell on you, Daddy?"

He grinned.

"Not that kind of spell. But I feel responsible for you."

"I believe that's known as parenting."

"One's child isn't supposed to look at you with adult eyes and say those things. I should've found you as a teenager."

"Yes, you should've. But I'll try to drum up some adolescent behavior, just for you."

"Do your worst. It has to be easier than what you've put me through the last few days."

"You haven't earned your stripes yet."

"Right. I'll earn them at dinner, when I apologize."

"And then for many years afterward, when you make certain not to lose me from your life again."

"Yes, dear. Now go get ready. I'm taking you to the fanciest restaurant in Kymi."

The next morning as the sun streamed in my room, I stood wrapped in a towel while I pondered what to wear. My father and I had talked for hours the night before, and he had told me about his reasons for staying away, and also how worthless those reasons seemed now. If I could forgive him, it would be more than he deserved.

I forgave him on the spot. One only has one father, and in truth, he'd put a spell on me. I wanted more of his time, and just like when I made Miklos my pen pal; I had every intention of getting it.

But now that the relationship with him was settled, I turned my mind to my next challenge. Miklos was coming to take me to a nice beach he'd heard about a few miles from Kymi, one that was beautiful but tended to be deserted.

There was really only one choice. I reached in my suitcase and pulled out the two small pieces of yellow and white striped fabric.

"Well, June," I muttered. "Time to use the big guns."

An hour later Miklos bumped us over the edge of the road on a motorcycle he'd borrowed from someone. He parked us, and we looked out from a small vantage point to view the aqua water that stretched out to meet a turquoise blue sky. We climbed off the motorcycle, and my new sundress fluttered in the wind.

But the air was warm, kissing my skin instead of chilling it. Miklos untied the bundles from the bike, one containing our towels and clothing, and the other holding our lunch. He propped them both over his shoulder and held out a hand.

We climbed down a rugged rock pile, but soon a triangle of deserted white sand greeted us. No more than a half-mile across, the big crowds drove right by it. The green hills of the island shielded it from view on both sides. I felt like it was a slice of beauty, set aside for me. And the man that made me the hungriest turned to let the wind ruffle his hair before angling his brown eyes down to look at me.

"Are you afraid, Therese?"

I blinked. On the contrary.

"Don't worry. We won't go out far, and I can teach you how to swim very well."

I gave him a slow grin.

"My life is in your hands," I said, kicking off my sandals and putting a dainty toe in the water. I waited until he had relaxed and was setting down his bundles before I pulled off my sundress, turning my head sideways to shake out my hair. I peeked, and held in a smile.

My yellow and white bikini had gotten the proper reaction.

He was staring, his mouth open for several seconds until he remembered to close it. I saw his neck muscles move as he swallowed.

"I thought I should reward you by wearing my new swimsuit," I said.

"It's going to be hard not to trifle with you while you're wearing that," he responded.

"That's the idea."

"Be careful, Pouli."

"Haven't you learned anything about me?"

"I've learned about you since you were ten-years-old and came to change my life forever."

"Forever?"

"Come on. You're trying to distract me, but I intend to teach you to swim."

"You'll have to catch me first!" I shouted, darting off.

We chased each other around for a while, and then he got me into the water. He was a patient teacher, and I laughed and tried to take him seriously.

But it was just too nice of a day, and he was too hard to resist. Soon I had him kissing me, as we stood up waist deep in the water.

"Therese," he said, in between contacts. "What is it you want?"

"What is it you want?" I countered.

"I think that's obvious."

I grabbed onto him, up on my toes. He kissed me until we were both quiet, conversation forgotten. But he never moved beyond. He touched my shoulders, my waist and my face and hands. I too, didn't push him. It was at that moment that I realized most how much I could trust him. Here in the deserted piece of beach, with the ancient Aegean Sea our only witness, he could've trifled all he wanted with the obviously willing American girl. There were only two possibilities as to why he didn't.

Either he wanted more from me and was willing to wait for the bigger promise of a fulfilled relationship, or he wasn't interested and had no deeper feelings than the desire of the moment and didn't want to use me and cast me away.

That thought brought me crashing back to Earth. I pulled my lips away, my hands trailing down the skin of his arms from his shoulders. I stared up at him, letting him see it all in my eyes, including my dawning disappointment. If he had wanted more from me, wouldn't he have spoken by now?

"Don't look at me like that, Pouli."

I blinked heavily and turned away. I didn't want him to see everything, like how much his rejection was going to hurt. Why hadn't I thought of that before? I hunched my shoulders and waded away from him, and got to the beach and my sundress, fumbling for it with shaking fingers.

But he was upon me in a few seconds, taking my arms in his hands.

"No, Therese! I don't mean to hurt you!"

"You're a good friend and a good man, all right? Now will you let me alone? I can find my own way back!"

"No!" he bellowed, his voice and his eyes filled with passion.

The amount of intensity on his face couldn't be ignored. I froze like a small ice crystal, vibrating in the heat of a ray of sun. His voice gentled.

"Don't you see why I'm waiting, Therese? Should I take hold of you now, when you've been sick, and lonely, and hurt by violence? Maybe you need to realize what it would be like with a man like me once you were strong again, one that has a small boat business with a friend and a funny little apartment in Heraklion."

"A man that I've longed to hear from since I was a child? A man who's saved my life and been my friend and made me ache for more?" I demanded. "I may have been sick and without a father and hurt, Miklos, but I'm not stupid! I know what I want, what I've wanted since the moment you picked me up at the airport!"

"You know what you want, eh?"

I grinned and stared at him like he was a monster plate of spaghetti and I had two forks. That got him. Soon he was crushing me to him, kissing me like a wild man, and running his hands up and down my back and shoulders but still stopping himself from going further with a roar of frustration.

At last I laughed at him.

"Well, do you want me or not?" I asked.

"I can't, Pouli. I can't take you like this. My parents would kill me, if I survived your father to reach them, that is. This is Greece, after all, and I've been raised old-fashioned."

We laughed, kissed some more, had some lunch, and then, when we sat on a blanket with our hands threaded together, declared our love to each other.

Chapter Twenty-Nine

Miklos proposed that very day. He even went and asked my father for his permission. His brother was told next, followed by a phone call to his parents. We told Andros and our other friends, assuring them that without their help we could've never made it. I wrote my mother a long letter, with an abbreviated version of the whole adventure in deference to her attention span. We began planning the wedding. A few days later I sat outside a small restaurant that was near my hotel room, with the Greek sunlight dappling the walls of a whitewashed stand of shops, and a gentle breeze stirring my hair. I had just picked up a letter from my mother and I tore it open.

Dear Therese,

Well, I guess I'm not too surprised that you're going to marry that Greek boy, especially after reading your story. You always did demand your own way, and I gave in to you. I know you think it was because I was a lazy mother, but to tell the truth, you were always smarter than me, and knew better than I what you needed. You got that intelligence from your father.

Xavier and I are coming, Pet, so don't get married without us. You seem to have gotten Austin under your thumb and so he's going to be there too. That will be awkward! I'm not sure what I should wear! But Xavier says that any man smart enough to marry me is worth his time, and he's willing to be pleasant to him. Can you believe this man I've married? He's still perfect, Therese, even on a cranky morning! I told him that Austin may have managed to marry me once, but he was the one who was able to keep me! I was wearing that small orange and turquoise blue mini dress when I said it to him; do you remember it? Xavier likes it, a lot. And from that you may draw whatever clues you need to keep your man interested.

You tell that boy that he's lucky to have you, from me, Pet. And don't worry! We'll have many a sun-filled vacation together in the future, when I make Xavier bring me to Greece often to visit. We can share bikinis!

June

I put her letter down and smiled to myself. The world was a small place to my mother, and melancholy was so dull. As I put the letter back in the envelope a smaller slip of paper fell out. It was another note she had written, a postscript on its own sheet. I felt a pang when I opened it.

Let's keep our little house, though, Therese, all right? Sometimes we'll go there, just you and me. We'll sit outside in the summer and try to get a tan, and we'll sit inside when it's raining and eat Malamars and dream.

I held that note up to the light, and looked at her teenager handwriting through a blur of tears. I was glad that no one was near me at the moment as I whispered out loud.

"We'll get together, June," I promised. "In our own little house. You'll see!"

I went back to my hotel determined to make my mother happy, my father happy, Miklos' family and friends happy, and then the man himself appeared as I turned the corner. He was leaned against the wall of my hotel, waiting for me, his silhouette slim in the shadows like the boy he had been once. And then he turned, and I stepped into the same shade and blended. His face lit in a bountiful grin and I reached out my two hands. He took them, and then, that gesture satisfied, drew me into his arms and hugged me. I learned then that I could have more than one home in the world. The one I left behind but determined to visit, and the one I made my own now.

It was a few days later, when I was preparing every day for my wedding, that the last surprising thing happened. I was alone in my hotel room, and someone knocked. Thinking it was Miklos I opened it with a smile on my face, but one glance at my visitor and the smile faded into shock.

Stubbo. Standing before me in a beige sports coat that had extra widths on the upper arm sleeves to fit his cement block muscles. I tensed, unable to choose what my reaction should be, when he held up a quick hand.

"Wait, don't scream," he said, but the tone of his voice surprised me as much as the fact that he knew how to speak. I clutched the door, putting it between us.

"What do you want?" I gasped.

"To give you this."

I looked down at his massive paw.

"My letters!"

I think of all the strange occurrences that had happened to me over the past few months, this one was the oddest. Stubbo and I had a nice little talk. It turned out that he wasn't such a bad guy; he was a real estate agent from Idaho. He bulked up to do weight lifting matches in his spare time. He'd been coerced into following me, due to a connection of malodorous bloodlines with a distant cousin. He didn't tell me what the evil scientists had threatened him with, but his job had been to follow me from Seattle to Athens, and make certain that I ended up on Thuggery Island.

He looked ashamed when he apologized for shaking me.

"And I'm sorry I tore your dress," he had added. I pointed out that if he had wanted to scare me into proceeding to my father's address, using words instead of just showing up and scaring me might have been more effective. Miklos shook his head when I told him about it later.

"And you believed everything he told you, I suppose," he accused.

"But Miklos, he said he was sorry!"

"Therese, he could be the worst gangster ever released on the Grecian Islands."

"Why track me down to apologize then?"

"Perhaps because you light fires under men."

"Fiddlesticks!"

"'Fiddlesticks?'"

"It means nonsense, balderdash!"

"Balder ..."

"You know what I mean! Besides, he gave me your letters back, Miklos. No man interested in me for himself would've done that."

"And why not? It gave him a perfect excuse to talk to you."

I sat beside him and snuggled in.

"Because anyone who read those letters would know that you were irresistible," I told him.

"I'm irresistible, eh, Pouli?"

"And I light fires under men."

"Our wedding night should be something special then."

"I can't wait."

I had the decency not to invite Stubbo to the wedding, but everyone else was there. Family, friends, hotel desk clerks, acquaintances, it was a large colorful party. I was there when my mother and father met again for the first time in 23 years. I was relieved to see no spark, and no lingering yearning for each other between them. My mother clung to her new husband, who was gracious. My father was calm and practical. He'd brought a date of his own, and I was dying of curiosity to know where he had produced her from. My first impression, however, is that it made my mother and my step-father more relaxed to see that he had an attachment of his own.

But soon I forgot my parents as I stood beside Miklos exchanging our vows. The wedding had both American and Grecian elements. My dress was what every trendy young woman of the seventies would like to wear, but also laden with enough fluff and lace to please my new mother-in-law. She and my mother, who hit it off just as well now as they had twelve years ago, spent a lot of time laughing together over the final preparations.

The next morning after all the celebrations were done, and the short burst of a nap we had taken among the revelers, Miklos and I set off in the small yacht he and Andros used to impress tourists with. It seemed that Xavier and my father had actually gotten together and paid to rent us a special honeymoon house on a near deserted island close to Skyros.

I loved the pleasant house right away, and I was relieved that the small island had a tiny population of its own. Too much isolation would've reminded me of my terror-filled night on Patismasia. A few shops, and tiny houses lined the track that led to our spot. As we walked the landscape became more piercing in its beauty, and more empty of other people. We found that the shoreline near our honeymoon home was deserted for miles. Miklos opened the door and we went inside to put down our cases and admire the bright and colorful rooms. Then we went outside to the sea. The mid-morning sun shone down on us as we stood on the beach and listened to the silence of a peace that had been hard won.

I closed my eyes and shivered with happiness and anticipation. This was our first moment alone since we'd gotten married. He had the same idea as he caught onto me and kissed me. He was too gentle and cautious so I grabbed hold tight, encouraging him to forget my recent illness and all that we'd been through. There was only this sensation, of taste and hunger and of my expensive tastes. We couldn't get close enough. He stopped to breathe after several minutes and dipped his forehead down to mine. I kissed his cheek, and his grip behind my waist tightened.

"Of all the people you light a fire under, Therese, I still can't believe that I'm the one that gets to have you," he said in my ear.

"Miklos, you're a monster plate of spaghetti."

He drew back and laughed.

"You have no sense of romance, Pouli."

"Come here and try to say that again."

"That look in your green eyes, I think I'm afraid," he replied. We backed away for a moment, holding our two hands and grinning into each other's faces.

I smiled and got down with my legs folded under me to dig in my beach bag and find some lotion. Taking off my sundress slow and shaking out my hair, I gave Miklos the first glimpse of the bikini my mother had bought for me in Athens on her way to the wedding. I saw him freeze in place as he stared, and then swallow heavily. He came and drew me to my feet. His face was intense with concentration.

He said something short and melodious in Greek, and I knew that he wasn't swearing at me now.

"You'd better not be offering me a swimming lesson," I said.

"Later, Pouli," he muttered.

• • •

Victoria Bastedo

Victoria Bastedo is an escape artist. From the time she was small in Kansas City, she's enjoyed vanishing into all forms of fiction, whether it occurs first in her daydreams, a book or a show. She also loves to walk and peruse landscapes and architecture, to socialize with her friends and to dabble with occasional arts and crafts. She's lived the best romance because she married a good man, and thanks God for her large family. An active member of her writing group, she recommends writers find others who share their dreams to enrich and support them.